PUFFIN BOOKS

JASON BODGER AND THE PRIORY GHOST

Jason Bodger doesn't realize just what he is letting himself in for when he visits an ancient local priory with Class 4z. After all, how was *he* to know that Mathilda de Chetwynde, born over 700 years ago, was going to latch on to him and haunt him unmercifully? Poor Jason's life can never be the same again as he becomes inextricably involved in riotous and hilarious escapades in this original, clever and very funny book.

Gene Kemp is the award-winning author of *The Turbulent Term of Tyke Tiler*, *Gowie Corby Plays Chicken* and *Charlie Lewis Plays for Time*. She used to be a teacher, is married with three children, and now has a granddaughter.

Other books by Gene Kemp

CHARLIE LEWIS PLAYS FOR TIME
THE CLOCK TOWER GHOST
DOG DAYS AND CAT NAPS
GOWIE CORBY PLAYS CHICKEN
NO PLACE LIKE
THE TURBULENT TERM OF TYKE TILER
DUCKS AND DRAGONS (ed.)

JASON BODGER AND THE PRIORY GHOST

Gene Kemp

Illustrated by
Elaine McGregor Turney

PUFFIN BOOKS
in association with
FABER AND FABER

PUFFIN BOOKS

Published by the Penguin Group
27 Wrights Lane, London W8 5TZ, England
Viking Penguin Inc., 40 West 23rd Street, New York, New York 10010, USA
Penguin Books Australia Ltd, Ringwood, Victoria, Australia
Penguin Books Canada Ltd, 2801 John Street, Markham, Ontario, Canada L3R 1B4
Penguin Books (NZ) Ltd, 182–190 Wairau Road, Auckland 10, New Zealand

Penguin Books Ltd, Registered Offices: Harmondsworth, Middlesex, England

First published by Faber and Faber 1985
Published in Puffin Books 1987
Reprinted 1988

Made and printed in Great Britain by
Richard Clay Ltd, Bungay, Suffolk

For Juliet and Penny

About this story

"I can't believe that!" said Alice.

"Can't you?" the Queen said in a pitying tone. "Try again; draw a long breath and shut your eyes."

Alice laughed. "There's no use trying," she said: "one can't believe impossible things."

"I dare say you haven't had much practice," said the Queen. "When I was your age, I always did it for half an hour a day. Why, sometimes I've believed as many as six impossible things before breakfast."

Lewis Carroll: *Through the Looking Glass*

Chapter One

One warm afternoon in early May when the trees were shoving out white, pink and red blossom as if the whole country was taking part in a giant Flower Festival, a school crocodile – no, not the man-eating variety, but the two-by-two, school-uniformed, anoraked, notebook-carrying, I'm-not-walking-with-you-Rodney-Bennet, so-get-lost; don't kick anyone walking in front, children; Jason Bodger, stop pushing other people; Anne Brontë, keep up with the other two; put away those sweets, Adam Bede; stop pushing, Jason Bodger; Mary Webb, there's nothing to cry about; behave yourself, Chrystal Ewing; Jason Bodger, don't you dare spit on a public pavement; and stop kicking, you'll get left behind next time there's an outing, in fact why I brought you with us today will ever remain a mystery to me – type of crocodile – made its way from the classroom to the inner part of a small city.

Mrs Cooper, the class teacher, strode along at its head, as fast as her little legs would allow, followed by members of Year 4 Class z, and bringing up the rear, trying to make his lanky legs fit in with the others, came Mr Pridmore, a long, thin and timid student rather like a tall rabbit. He was growing a scanty little ginger bristly beard to make him less nervous and he wore contact lenses so that he shouldn't have to worry about wearing glasses. He worried about losing his contact lenses instead.

Mr Pridmore loved children and wanted to teach more than anything in the whole world. He was a very nice person, Mr Pridmore. He wanted them to call him Anthony, but this just made them giggle. It was just a pity that he'd landed Year 4 Class z on his teaching practice. Year 4 Class x and Year 4 Class y were both much pleasanter for they didn't have Jason Bodger.

Mr Pridmore had nights when he couldn't sleep for thinking of Jason Bodger. Before he went on teaching practice he hadn't known that anywhere in the world existed anybody or anything like Jason Bodger. But he knew now. And sometimes he felt that he would never be the same again.

Actually, after this day neither would Jason Bodger. But that's the next part of the action.

For the moment Year 4 Class z were walking along on the warm and beautiful beginning of summer, happy to be out of school and on a History outing. Mr Pridmore's main subject was History, and they'd been studying life in the Early Middle Ages under the Plantagenet Kings. "The who?" asked Jason Bodger. "Never 'eard of 'em." They'd read, written, talked about, drawn and taped lots of stuff about A Day in the Life of . . . A Rich Lord in a Castle, A Poor Boy Working on the Land, One of King Richard's Crusaders, and so on. Jason Bodger said what he wanted was a Day in the Life of a Man-eating, Rabid Sabre-toothed Tiger, and refused to believe they didn't exist in the Middle Ages.

"Well, gimme a Day in the Life of a Blood-sucking Vampire Bat in one of them Castles," he offered. "That'd be all right."

"Impossible," sniffed Phrynne* Jamieson, who was too clever by half or even three-quarters. "It would have to be a Night in the Death of a Blood-sucking Vampire. Be logical."

At this point Mr Pridmore rapped his desk, a desperate look in his eyes.

"We are here to discuss the Middle Ages, not vampires," he cried.

"That's a pity," said Jason, "very int'resting, vampires. I tell you what, Sir, I'll lend you my magazines on 'orror and witchcraft. They'll teach you a lot about vampires and such like int'resting things, Mr Pridmore. You'll like them. I'll bring them for you tomorrow."

"No, thank you," shuddered Mr Pridmore. "Now can we go on with our next Day in the Life of . . ."

"Tarzan in Sherwood Forest?" suggested Jason, helpfully.

"It wasn't Tarzan in Sherwood Forest," cried Mr Pridmore. "It was Robin Hood."

"Oh, Robin 'ood will do. Tarzan meets Robin 'ood in Sherwood Forest."

Eventually they got down to work on A Day in the

*Pronounced "Frin". Some people called her Frynay which she hated.

Life of a Monk or a Nun in the Middle Ages, and after a very long afternoon, Mr Pridmore was able to get back to his college room and write up his notes in his teaching practice file. "Despite all my work and preparation this lesson was not a great success," he wrote, before retiring to bed with three aspirins and a hot whisky.

However, several children came up to him next day and told him they'd enjoyed it and his spirits lifted.

"Coming on. You're coming on," boomed Mrs Cooper. "What about a little outing to finish it all off? There's a small Priory in town. One can look round it."

So there they were. Off to see it. Till the last moment Mr Pridmore kept hoping that Jason would catch measles or break his ankle on the way to school. But no. He appeared, smiling and horribly healthy. Then Mr Pridmore tried to find the courage to make him stay at school while the rest went. But he was a kind and hopeful man and when Jason pushed his face up close and said, "I ain't 'alf lookin' forward to this arternoon and visiting them nuns, Sir," he hadn't the heart to say:

"Stay at school, Bodger, and copy out sixty pages from your History book," which secretly he would have liked to do.

"Glad you're looking forward to it, Jason. So am I," he lied, instead.

They had to cross a murderous road where fiendish motorists, apparently practising for the Grand Prix, seemed to be trying to score points on how close they could shave a pedestrian without actually hitting one. Parents paled at the thought of their loved little ones crossing this particular road. Petitions were constantly being signed for a pedestrian crossing.

Undismayed by the hurtling traffic, Mrs Cooper strode on her short legs into the middle of the road, holding up a huge multi-coloured umbrella. Brakes screeched, horns hooted, but there was that something about Mrs Cooper which could bring even an articulated container lorry driven by a bad-tempered Frenchman to a halt. She gestured with an arm and Class 4z scuttled across followed by Mr Pridmore in an acute state of nerves. Jason Bodger stuck out his tongue, and waggled his fingers at all the waiting traffic. One tired lorry driver who had been on the road for many hours held back his vehicle with difficulty at the sight, but they all reached the other side safely, so Mrs Cooper furled up her brolly and on they went, Mrs Cooper sailing ahead like a flag-ship.

It grew hotter as they went along. Anoraks were peeled off. Jason handed his to Mr Pridmore to carry. Then past the cinema, with Jason stopping to admire a poster of a lady wearing as little as possible.

"Caw," he said, but Mrs Cooper tapped him with her long umbrella and they moved on through a park, going crazy with spring and blossoming flowers, in the centre of which stood an old ruined castle, covered with moss. It looked cool and refreshing as did the nearby stream flowing into a pool, and the children wanted to stop but were moved on by Mrs Cooper's umbrella. Then they passed through an archway out of the park and into narrow streets.

"These are the oldest streets in the city," said Mr Pridmore. "They date right back to the Middle Ages."

"Look how narrow they are," cried Mrs Cooper. "Jason Bodger, stop kicking Hilary and look at THE NARROW STREETS."

"She ain't got four eyes, she's got six, two at the front, two at the back and one over each ear," Jason muttered to his friend Sam, walking beside him.

The street grew even narrower if possible. It was one they all knew well because it ran just behind Woolworths, Marks and Sparks and British Home Stores, but the same places seem quite different when you're out with the school, not shopping with your mum. The tops of the building stuck out further than the bottoms, which had very expensive small shops fitted into them.

"Mr Pridmore," bellowed Jason in his loud gruff voice.

"Yes?"

"Is this where they used to empty the chamber pots out of the windows on to the people walking below? Like you told us?"

Several people looked round at this interesting question.

"Well . . . er . . . yes," said Mr Pridmore.

"People with bad manners and habits, Jason Badger," called out Mrs Cooper.

"Well . . . really . . . it was everybody . . ." said Mr Pridmore.

"I think we'd better go on."

They turned a corner. The street became an alleyway for pedestrians only.

And suddenly the Priory was in front of them, square in shape, not very tall, built of reddish stone with big chimneys and tiny windows. There was no drive approaching it. The Priory's heavy wooden door opened straight out of the alleyway. Mr Pridmore felt happy at last. He was delighted with it. He could show his class, all dear children at heart, the delights of this quaint building and transport them back with him to another age, so that they'd learn to love History as he did.

Jason Bodger was less impressed.

"That ole place," he said. "I know *that*. Fancy coming 'ere. Fought it was an ole barn or garage or summat. I fought we'd see summat like Dracula's castle in Transylvania – y'know, all them mountains and foggy mist, and precipes and battlements and things wiv vampires and spooks leaping about."

"What, here? In the middle of the city?" sniffed Phrynne.

Jason sank into a deep gloom. He could see this expedition was going to be dead boring. On the other hand, they weren't in school. He and Sam could make something of it. He fished in his pocket for some chewing gum, and gave Hilary Jenkins an encouraging shove just at the back of his knee. Hilary Jenkins was a nerd thought Jason (doubtless caused by being given a girl's name) and needed to be shaken up occasionally just to let him know he was in the land of the living.

Mrs Cooper strode over to the curator, who handed out a roll of tickets. The necessary money had been paid earlier. Class 4z looked round. They were in a large low room, cool and dark, with fat stone pillars, a tiny window and a large wooden chest.

"Two other schools here," said the curator. "Do you want me to show you round or do you want to do it on your own?"

"Get off that chest, Jason Bodger. You're disturbing all the leaflets," said Mrs Cooper, using the eyes at the back of her head.

"There are some things I'd especially like to point out to the children," put in Mr Pridmore.

"I think we'll have the guide," Mrs Cooper smiled. Mr Pridmore did not.

"Ain't there no gift shop then?" asked Chrystal Ewing.

"No," snapped Mrs Cooper. "You're here to feel the atmosphere and get an idea how people lived in earlier times."

"I wanted a gift for me mum. Don't seem much point in coming without a gift shop," went on Chrystal Ewing.

"There's a very strong atmosphere here," said Phrynne to her friend, Harriet.

"I find it creepy," agreed Harriet.

"If you mean it stinks," said Jason, "it's them old pots over there. Stick your nose in one. Summat definitely croaked in there."

"I'm not at all sure I like it here," muttered Hilary Jenkins, "and I don't think we should have come."

"I reckon it's great then," said Jason heartily. Anything Hilary didn't like, he did, automatically.

"Come along, children," said the curator, "and we'll begin our little tour. This is a tiny place and . . ."

No one was taking any notice.

"Class 4z . . ." cried Mrs Cooper. Everyone took notice and the tour began.

They went through a door.

"The Benedictine Priory of St Katherine's was founded late in the eleventh century, some twenty years after the Norman Conquest, and dedicated to the Church of St Katherine's in the High Street. In the park nearby, to the north, the stream which supplied the water for all their needs still flows. It was known as 'The Minchin Lake', or the Nun's Brook. . . ."

At this point Jason blanked off. They were in . . .

"The Crypt," said the curator. Jason brightened. That was better. Crypt didn't have a bad sound. And the pillars were very wide and squat. He slid behind one, pulling Sam with him. He and Sam would do the tour on their own. Much more interesting. Bound to be some torture machines somewhere f'rinstance. Surely someone came in and tortured these old nuns from time to time. They did in those days. Always doing the odd bit of torture, when they weren't galloping round the countryside or living in forests or dying of plague.

"Look at them barmy girls over there," whispered Sam. "Must be one of them other schools."

"Funny uniform they're wearing. Look like old bats, don't they?" said Jason.

"I've got some peanuts."

"Givuss some then."

"King John and his Queen Isabella visited here. He was very generous to this Priory," the curator said.

"Wicked King John?" asked Phrynne.

"That all depends," cried Mr Pridmore, determined to have some say. "Sometimes people weren't as bad as history records."

"I wanted a gift shop," said Chrystal Ewing.

"Jason Bodger, come out from behind that pillar," said Mrs Cooper. "And hand over those peanuts, Sam Stokes."

"Now we are proceeding upstairs to the first floor," announced the curator.

The staircase was narrow and winding, though Jason managed to find room to jab Hilary quite gently.

"The spook's got you," he hissed in his ear so that poor Hilary would have leapt half a mile in the air only there wasn't sufficient space on the stairs which were further crowded by a class from one of the other schools coming down as they went up led by the curator's part-time assistant, who hated the curator and school parties fairly equally. Jason wanted to go through a small door on the left but was told that it led on to the roof and wasn't safe. Disappointed, he followed the class through a large dining hall of incredible dullness, followed by a bedroom containing a huge fourposter and a cradle with a doll in it over which there were some gooings. Jason made sick noises. Really this was boring. He'd be almost glad to get back to school.

"Are you all right, Hilary? You look pale," said Mrs Cooper.

"I don't like it here. I do wish I hadn't come," Hilary moaned.

"Take a deep breath and think happy thoughts, child. Then if you don't feel better I'll take you outside. Though I must say, I don't think there's any atmosphere here."

Phrynne spoke. "I feel something, Mrs Cooper."

"Let the past reach out to you," cried Mr Pridmore.

"That's all right to a certain extent but we have to live now," snapped Mrs Cooper, then turned to the curator. "Shall we go on?"

They arrived at another winding staircase at the top of which there was a large opening with a railing in front of it, like a balcony and looking over they could see the kitchen far below. Jason cheered up for the cooking utensils were the nearest things to torture instruments he'd seen as yet.

But what really caught his eye and held his attention was a huge dark beam, roughly shaped as if giant medieval jaws had chopped chunks from it, and on this beam but some distance away lay a higgledy-piggledy heap of paper cups and plates covered with bits and dust.

Jason nudged Sam.

"Them ole nuns must've 'ad some party sitting out there on that beam."

And he rummaged in his pockets for a pebble to throw at the plates and send them floating down to the kitchen fifty feet below.

The curator was speaking.

"That beam is all that remains of the dorter or dormitory. It would have been part of the floor. From the holes in the wall opposite you can see where there must once have been another beam."

Jason's fingers found not a stone but an old gunged sweet, took aim, threw and missed the plates as something slid into view, ruining his aim. The sweet pinged on a vast cauldron below, the class leaned forward to watch and Mrs Cooper hissed through her teeth, "Jason Bodger . . ." as the curator droned on.

Jason snarled to himself. He rarely missed anything. It was all the fault of some daft girl walking across the other beam. Her stupid uniform floating about had spoiled his shot. Or else her waving at him like that. What was she doing, anyway? He looked round at the class. They didn't appear to have noticed. He looked back at the girl. She smiled at him, nodded and waved again. At him. Yes, definitely at him.

And something dawned on him. Something that caused his stomach to leap up to his chin, then sink to his boots. Never mind the plates. This girl was walking towards him on a beam that wasn't there. This horrible girl, beaming, oh no, all over her face was walking on air. And coming for him, Jason Bodger.

Chapter Two

Back a bit. About eight hundred years give or take a few seasons. And, of course, in those days seasons did what they were supposed to do (ask anybody over thirty). Gentle breezes blew in spring, daffodils danced, blossoms bloomed, flowers flourished promptly as soon as March 21st came round. In summer it was hot, people made hay and turned brown, wore sun bonnets and lay under the greenwood trees drinking cider and home-brewed lemonade. In the middle of September, bang, there'd be a terrific thunderstorm, striking several old trees that needed felling anyway, and then autumn would blow in, whirling red, green, brown, orange, yellow, tawny, gold – no, not pink and blue, stupid – leaves into the air, while the forests wrapped themselves in mists so thick you couldn't see your hand in front of your face, if you ever wanted to. And in winter, the snow lay miles high, and people skated and roasted oxen on frozen lakes – to say nothing of venison if the lord was absent and his gamekeepers not looking. Venison is deer meat and very dear it proved if you were caught red-handed – you paid for it with your life.

Think to yourself about what they didn't have in Ye Merrie Englande. They didn't have:

computers, television
nuclear bombs
cars and planes
bicycles and trains
fridges and cookers
coke and ice cream
nuclear bombs
pesticides
radio, hospitals
fish and chips, burgers
not even potatoes
still waiting for Christopher Columbus to bring 'em
football or supermarkets
cigarettes
still waiting for Walter Raleigh to start smoking
bricks or chocolate
nuclear bombs
washing powder, toothpaste
and no electric light in winter when it got dark early and stayed that way for hours and hours and hours and hours with only a little candle to keep the big night outside at bay . . .

no biros nor lipsticks, penicillin, batteries, bathrooms, lavatories,
Prime ministers, policemen,
roller skates, taps . . .

no books . . . only a few.
no school . . . no school . . . no school . . .

except for the sons of kings and lords who were taken away from home at the age of seven to another castle where they learnt not to cry for their mothers or their nurses and to be a MAN – in those days a squire, then a knight.

Oh yes, they did have some places quite like school: monasteries, nunneries and priories.

*Imagine a forest, an enormous, huge, gigantic, immense, tremendous forest stretching and stretching on and on like a green blanket over all the country, with trees of oak, ash, beech and elder, holly, elm and hawthorn, and all around ivy and bracken and nettles and brambles and bluebells and cowslips and violets and primroses and buttercups and daisies and dandelions and fools' parsley and wild garlic and Jack-by-the-hedge and pig-nuts and mosses and lichen and grasses and herbs and celandines . . . and beetles and dragonflies and bees and wasps and wrens and robins and hawks and caterpillars and snakes and mice and voles and moles and hedgehogs and rabbits and squirrels (the red kind still as the grey ones hadn't yet arrived to drive them out), and stoats and weasels, and the big animals – for the woods were truly wild then – deer and badgers and foxes and wolves and the boar with its sharp killer tusks. Sometimes even a bear, though it was usually a poor shabby thing in chains, half-tame and tormented for the entertainment of the peasants.

*Get through as quick as poss, so you can read the good bits.

Here and there in this great green blanket forest were clearings where men had panted and sweated and grunted and laboured to make a bit of space for a few thatched houses of wattle and daub*, a little church and a massive castle for the Lord of the Manor as he was called, usually on a hill, a higher piece of ground with a moat round it and pike swimming in the water and a drawbridge that could be pulled up and down. In times of danger the villagers would take shelter in the castle with all their hens, pigs, children etc. and the drawbridge would be pulled up.

The Lord of the Manor was all-powerful and in our particular village belonging to Castle Adamant the people were grateful that theirs was kind by nature, a man called Sir Oswald de Chetwynde. His uncle, the lord before him, Sir Ranulf de Chetwynde, had been a wicked tyrant whose idea of Saturday night entertainment – you must remember he hadn't got telly so he couldn't watch people suffering in quizzes or competition games – was to string up someone and slowly roast him or her, beginning at the toes. He said it added to the quality of his evening meal, though it did little for the quality of life of the villagers. Eventually he was killed in mysterious circumstances while boar-hunting in the forest. Officially the boar got him but he was wearing several spears at the time. He looked like a hedgehog.

But Oswald, his nephew, who succeeded to the castle and estate, was a kind old soul, helping with the harvest, visiting the sick, settling disputes, treating

*Ask your teacher or any other grown-up hanging about.

chilblains, giving harvest feasts and inviting folk to sample his home-brew. The villagers hoped he'd live for ever, but he was getting on for those days when people died young, despite not eating junk food nor smoking.

But his wife kept having daughters, eight so far, and they couldn't inherit the place, sorry, girls.

So everyone wanted the Lady Ælfrida, as she was called, to have a son who would inherit the castle, or else it would go to another branch of the family, headed by Antacill de Chetwynde, even more beastly and cruel than old Ranulf.

Lady Æ. just had to have a son.

Now at the point we're arriving at, slowly, sorry, I'll hurry it up, it was a bitterly cold winter's night, branches iced up in the forest, everywhere iced up in Castle Adamant, cold at the best of times, a still and frosty December 31st, Old Year's Night or New Year's Eve, whichever you fancy, and the village folk wassailing and carrying on generally, keeping up the Twelve Days of Christmas Misrule they used to enjoy then, and poor Lady Æ. was having her ninth.

It was born on the stroke of midnight.* Sir Oswald, the ladies-in-waiting, the nurse, the midwife, and various attendants all rushed forward, hope in their hearts.

Sir Oswald turned away, a tear slipping down his cheek. One of the ladies began to sob.

"Oh no, not again," sighed the Lady Ælfrida, and died quietly with no fuss at all, but then she'd never been any trouble to anyone.

*Only there wasn't one.

The baby girl was roaring its head off and kicking. She was a strong baby. No one showed any interest.

"Don't ever let me see it," said Sir Oswald and strode out of the door, summoning his horse and servant so that he could ride away and join any particular old Crusade going on at that time.

But the old cook, Fat Johanna, whom everyone thought was past it (she was thirty-six), gathered the baby to her.

"It's not your fault, littl'un, me dayesye. I'll look after 'ee."

Chapter Three

Jason didn't care for the look of this girl at all. He wouldn't have done even if she hadn't been bearing down on him across a beam that wasn't there. She looked like a bat in her queer clothes and he couldn't see her hair as it was wrapped up in a pudding cloth or something similar. But her face was coming nearer and nearer and he didn't like it. Jason, when he took any notice of girls at all, which wasn't often, liked them pretty. And gentle. And quiet. With big eyes and long eyelashes that fluttered when he, Jason, laid down the law as he often did in the classroom, which was quite right and proper since he was bigger than anyone else, better at games than anyone else, and as for work, he could come top if he wished but he'd more important things to do all the time. About once a term, though, Jason would take a fancy to a girl for a few days. She always had curls and a giggle and big eyes as we've said before, and knew her place. Actually, Phrynne Jamieson was much the prettiest girl in the class but she had no idea of her place at all. Stuck up and bossy was Phrynne Jamieson. Besides, Jason couldn't spell her name and she laughed at him.

The girl was very near now and something about her was sending a nasty, prickly, tickling, itchy feeling down Jason's spine, causing his toes to curl and his thumbs to prick horribly. It may have been her grin – all those teeth – surely she'd got more than her fair share? Maybe it was her pale face with all those freckles – she'd definitely got more than her fair share. Maybe it was her fierce blue eyes – almost purple – and glittering, maybe it was her long pale eyelashes – she was near enough now for him to see them – that so often go with red hair. Jason preferred blondes, blue eyes, glinting curls. Part of Phrynne Jamieson's trouble was that she had black hair – straight – that just curled at the ends. This girl was worse, no hair – just a cloth. But Jason knew that underneath it was red. He'd known this girl for a long time, he felt suddenly, but that was ridiculous. He'd never seen her before in his life and to tell the truth he could have quite happily gone on that way. He didn't feel she was going to add anything to it at all. Then he clutched Sam, feeling sick and dizzy as everything seemed to slide away into a muzzy blur, the Priory, the stone walls, the voice of the guide, Mrs Cooper and Mr Pridmore, the footsteps of the children and the visitors, Sam chewing gum (a loud gum-chewer, Sam), Hilary whimpering about something . . .

"Who is she? What does she want?" he managed to whisper.

Sam unhitched the hand clutching him.

"Sam, why is she coming for me?"

"Look," said Sam, from some far-distant shore,

Africa or China say, "I've offered you some gum three times. D'you want it or not?"

The girl had nearly reached him now, smiling and nodding her head and talking double Dutch. Yes, definitely double Dutch. Jason couldn't make out a word of it. Not that he was at all sure he wanted to, but she did give him this feeling – very strongly indeed – that what she was saying in double Dutch was very, very important, might even be the most important thing that ever happened to Jason Bodger.

She stepped off the beam that wasn't there and up some steps that weren't there either and through the open space towards Jason.

"Sam. Listen. Who is she?"

"What the heck are you rabbiting on about?"

She was close now, mouthing incomprehensible sounds, her bony little hands outstretched towards him.

"What do you want?" he whispered. The eagerness in her face terrified him.

"Pack it in," hissed Sam. "You look nutty, standing there gibbering to yourself."

"You speak to her," pleaded Jason.

"Oh come on. Stop messing about."

Sam pulled at his sleeve. So did she. Jason thought he might be going out of his mind. And then was sure of it as Sam moved and stepped right through the girl. Who vanished.

Chapter Four

Sunlight in a clearing; bright green, unpolluted grass soft and velvety as moss, sprigged with daisies, and all about the green leaves of the forest stretching all around, around, around for ever: the forest the world, all the world the forest.

The Lady Mathilda Isabel Alys de Chetwynde rolled on the daisies and waggled her dirty legs in the air. Usually she wore old bits of cloth wrapped round them, Middle-Aged leg-warmers you could say, but today was warm and she'd flung them off. And she was dirty because she didn't wash. They didn't much in those days. They were a grotty lot – not like the Romans always having baths – your medieval ancestors and mine. And she liked rolling on the daisies because they sprang back afterwards. Buttercups didn't. Violets didn't. Celandines flattened themselves sensibly. Bluebells and cowslips broke. The thin delicate windflowers died.

"Nesch," screamed Mathilda. "Ich loue dayeseyes,"* and rolled down a slope colliding with a

*"Softly. I love daisies."

boy sharpening a stick with a knife that your museum would gloat over if you dug it up in your back garden today. Beside him lay a large whippet-thin dog, and Mathilda finally crashed on to his ribs.

"Gode Perry," she cried and he licked her face. Almost anyone else he would have torn in half, for he was an alaunt and they weren't nice dogs. They weren't meant to be in those days, for people didn't have pretty little pets with ribbons in their topknots and jewelled collars, eating out of tins and being taken for a five-minute walk in the park twice a day. These dogs were for hunting and fighting and guarding, and Peredoc was no exception. But it was the boy who made the growling noise, for Mathilda's larking about had nearly caused him to stab himself with the knife. The noise he made could be understood anywhere, any time, a universal shout of push off, get lost, scram, scarper, skedaddle, vamoose, shove off and lots of other words I'm not allowed to write down here.

From a nearby tree a cuccu – I mean cuckoo – sang and set Mathilda off again.

*"Sumer is icumen in;**
Lhude sing cuccu!
Groweth sed, and bloweth med,
And springeth the wude nu.
Sing cuccu, cuccu, cuccu."

This may not sound like Number One in the charts to you, but it was in those days. Minstrels would wander from castle to castle throughout the country

*This may not be the exact song she sang but it was something like that.

playing and singing, bringing songs and news, and they were jolly popular (if they were any good), and would be paid with food and drink and prezzies and lodging for the night, and if they weren't any good they probably had bones and rotten eggs and worse thrown at them not to mention cat-calls and kicks. No, they didn't take their electric guitars or their synthesizers with them – they played – come to think of it, what did they play? Blowed if I know.* Back to old Mathilda.

Incidentally, if you're having trouble with Mathilda's language, I'm sorry, for I know Middle English isn't the easiest thing in the world, though you can be grateful she didn't speak Old English or Anglo-Saxon, much, much worse, with some terrible-looking letters in it called thorns (I ask you) looking like p's gone barmy. Actually, since she was a jokey girl, some of the corny old jokes you hear today were probably told by her eight hundred years ago. Yes, that's why they sound so old. They are.

That day in the clearing, with Jos, her friend, and Perry, the dog, Mathilda was happy. She usually was. And I hope this is a relief to you, because in nearly all the stories I've read about long ago, people are dead miserable. Have you noticed? It's always cold; bleak winds are blowing over the thin ice (you'd think it was Siberia) as bitter snow falls. Great World-shattering Events are happening and the children, all very sad and cold, are not only mixed up in them but alter them in some *momentous* and *important* way, whether it's

*What would the latest group or Lennon or Bowie have played if they'd been around in Mathilda's time?

plague or the Fall of the Roman Empire or the Great Fire of London.

I promise you – cross my heart and hope somebody else dies – that as you read this book, you won't learn anything useful at all, that nobody will be cold or miserable for too long, please, and nothing *important* will happen, nothing that couldn't happen to me or you or even awful Chrystal Ewing at any time, that there'll be lots of pleasant and horrible happenings and surprises (why don't you think up a few?) but none of them will change *the world* or *the history of our country*. There, that's settled. Where were we? Back to our Mathilda, she of the Dirty Legs warbling about cuccus and annoying Jos. Jos was serious-minded. He was the son of Max, Mathilda's Dad's reeve or steward, who looked after the castle estate. And you've guessed it, of course, clever kids that you are, Mathilda is the baby who arrived a couple of chapters ago, who ought to have been a boy; Johanna's Day-esye, now aged eleven, twelve or thirteen or so, not that she knew or cared. At that moment in the sunshine she was a piece of power, she could do anything and everything, leap in the air, fly to the stars, live for ever. She flung her arms wide, whizzing round faster and faster till she fell on Jos *again* so that he nearly stabbed himself with his sharpened stick this time.

"Gon! Grobelly, rubelly, yobelling, noffling ninny bog!" he shouted. "Frittin' crittues for allwhere, evrywhere."

Work that one out and I'll go back to Standard Comprehensive and Primary Middle English for ever, promise.

And Jos pushed her away. Perry snarled at him but Mathilda biffed him on the nose and he subsided.

Jos finished sharpening his stick and stood up ready to start work, visiting various traps to see if there were any animals in them that could be carried back for meal-time at the castle, for in its way the forest was a supermarket. Jos and Mathilda didn't get upset about the animals for there wasn't much point, and after all Phrynne Jamieson, eight hundred years later on a Sunday outing, cried out with delight at the little lambs skipping in the springtime field until reminded by her father that it was to be roast lamb for dinner, whereupon she cried quite differently, but this didn't stop her enjoying it later. In fact she had two helpings.

Mathilda and Jos and Peredoc ran deeper into the forest which they knew so well, because they spent a lot of time there. Jos was a big strong lad with a lot of common sense and not much imagination. Mathilda was fierce and sharp one day, gentle the next, and her imagination was bigger than she was. Jos never noticed anyway, being too busy thinking about *things*: hunting, trapping, his weapon collection, planning for a peregrine, could he have one, after all he wasn't noble, only the son of the reeve (if he'd been noble he'd 've been in some other castle elsewhere) but he still wanted one. Mathilda didn't wish for *things*. She only wanted to be free and happy. And since the only people who took much notice of her were Fat Johanna and Jos, she was free and happy most of the time.

Her sisters treated her like dirt, noses (big ugly noses mostly) in the air, skirts drawn aside. No, they were not going to help in bringing up Mathilda like a lady. Her father had said he didn't want to set eyes on her again and they felt the same way, all of these boring girls, Margaret, Christianna, Cecilia, Eleanor, Avelina, Julietta, Adela and Bertha. Eleanor was the best of them; Avelina was an absolute toad (I don't know why toads should be absolute).

So Mathilda, lucky girl, missed out on all those womanly skills: sewing, weaving, embroidery, cooking, baking, making butter, skinning dead animals, singing and playing the lute, organizing prayers, tending illnesses, growing herbs, candle-making etc.

Instead she ran wild in the forest, climbing trees, learning to wrestle with Segg, the forester's lad, built like a tank with legs like tree-trunks, swimming in the moat in summer, skating on it in winter, except when she was with Fat Johanna in the kitchen stuffing herself. And at night she snuggled up to the comfortable fatnesses of Johanna in her bed covered with smelly furs, topped with that even smellier fur, Peredoc, and they were all like hot toast.

Later that afternoon she and Jos returned with a couple of dead animals and a few birds, to find excitement, bustle and hustle in the kitchen. Sir Oswald would be home soon, bringing guests with him. Mathilda and Jos were immediately roped in to perform various tasks, but there were so many people rushing hither and yon that Mathilda soon had enough, and she slipped quietly away to the roof, an exciting place to be, shortly followed by Jos, and they perched together on the parapet. From there you could look out over the miles of forest and up and away to the mountains in the distance. What Mathilda was watching was the woodland ride through the trees which Sir Oswald and his guests would probably take.

Jos wasn't interested in this. He'd got weapon mania and was working out how he would defend the castle from any enemies: drawbridge pulled up; a great log on the portcullis to squash them flat if they got across the moat; then if they got past that, a trap-door in the floor to drop them back into the moat; slits in the wall for arrows, spears and anything else; and finally boulders and cauldrons of boiling oil on the roof ready to be chucked over.

But Mathilda was gazing at the forest which, only a month ago, stood colourless and bare, grey and dismal. But now with the blue sky and the green leaves, the warm thatch of the villagers' cottages, the flowers and the hawthorn in blossom, the whole picture was like the tiny paintings that can be seen in the Duc de Berry's Book of Hours*. And soon the colours of Sir Oswald and the approaching company would add to it all.

"Sumer is icumen in. Llude sing cuccu," sang Mathilda, full of happiness. Make the most of it, old girl, for hard times are coming.

For one of those guests even then appearing in the far, far distance of the woodland ride was Sir Antacill, your friend and mine – to say nothing of the villagers'. And he was about to make an offer of marriage to any of the sisters, well, three had already gone, but Eleanor, Avelina, Julietta, Adela and Bertha were still available. The last two were a bit young but no one bothered about that in those days, and Julietta was not quite right in the head, but that wouldn't matter either. No one mentioned Mathilda. Not then. Sir Antacill and Sir Oswald had run into one another by chance and had a little chat about the future of the estate. Sir Antacill confessed his worry about the dowries yet to be paid out for all those girls. Marrying him would save on a dowry and provide for one of them, he said. Sir Oswald agreed he had a point there, especially when Sir Antacill pointed out that they were big ugly girls who ate a lot – something would have to

*Find out.

be done about them. He thought Eleanor was perhaps the least ugly, as far as he remembered. Should he take a look at Eleanor? Sir Oswald, a kindly man except where Mathilda was concerned, didn't like hearing his girls spoken of in such a way, but was forced to agree that it made sense, particularly since Antacill combined a smooth tongue with his vile nature. Together they headed for Our Castle.

The next few days were hectic. Feasting and hunting went on non-stop, to keep them all entertained, while the marriage negotiations got under way. And here 'orrible Anck, as he was now called by all the common people in the castle, ran into difficulties. For when the news was broken to Eleanor, she made a very loud noise, like an old train letting off steam – only they didn't recognize it because steam trains hadn't yet happened – and passed out rather noisily, going bump, bump, bump down those horrid stone stairs, since she had been standing at the top of them at the time. Of course, she was then out of commission for a few days, with bruises all over, several grazes, and an egg on her head. So everyone rode away and did yet more hunting till she recovered, nursed by Fat Johanna, who kept muttering, "Men." In case you haven't already realized, Fat Johanna was a Woman's Libber, born eight centuries ahead of time.

Which might account for the fact that when, a week later, Sir Oswald and Sir Antacill approached the bedroom of the Fair Eleanor – who really was not at all bad-looking, with lots of pretty hair and a nice nose – she wasn't there.

Oh, there was a to do. Oh, there was a carrying on.

The racks were brought out and various hot irons and so on, someone remembered the thumbscrew. They tortured* Segg and they wanted to torture Fat Johanna as well, but she just stood there, all fourteen stone of her and said, in that case there'll be no food for I'm the only one who can make that fire draw properly and work the spit. (No, stupid, not that kind of draw, nor that kind of spit, but you can find out what kind if you like.)

So they left Fat Johanna alone. Sir Antacill liked his grub. Next frantic searchings went on, through the castle, the church and all the wattle and daubs. This was particularly unfair as it was spring-cleaning time, and the women had just tidied up their homes, and the men had started on what small gardens they were allowed when Sir Antacill's soldiers came trampling over everything with their dirty boots. One housewife sent them packing with her broom, but they took it out on the next house by burning it down just to show them. But no joy, or rather no Eleanor. She'd gone, 'opped it, over the hills and far away, with a young trainee squire, doing a sort of Youth Opportunities Scheme at the Castle. Now in those days when the lord went away to the Crusades, the squire was always supposed to take a fancy to the lady, and play his harp or whatever and sing courtly songs to her while she did embroidery for hours on end, poor thing.

Well, this squire who was called Robyn (they were always called Robyn) hadn't got a lady for she'd died

*He'd pulled a face at 'orrible Anck and besides he **always** copped it. Fat Johanna nursed him better.

having our Mathilda, so he transferred all that love and longing to Eleanor the good-looker of the girls. Which is why she fell into a swoon (smashing word, swoon) when she was told she had to marry 'orrible Anck as her heart was already given to Robyn. Aided and abetted by Fat Johanna, she climbed out of one of the many castle slits down a rope to the waiting squire and rode away with him to Wales where his Dad, who was away fighting, owned a castle which Robyn looked after till Dad didn't come back from the Crusades, whereupon Robyn and Eleanor took over and lived happily ever after and had twelve children, and that's someone in the story settled happily, thank goodness.

"I'll 'ave 'im," said Toad Avelina. She meant Sir Antacill. "I've always wanted to be Lady of the Manor. I don't mind how horrible he is. Or how ugly."

"Well, you couldn't, could you?" said Mathilda, who just happened to be passing at the time.

"Don't you dare come near me, you maggoty, faggoty, murdering torment," shrieked Avelina, "or I shall put Tirrell the Terror on to you. And his hounds."

All this in Middle English, of course, and sounding even nastier than it does here. Tirrell was the cruellest of Sir Antacill's soldiers.

"Get knotted, big conk," replied Mathilda, sticking out her tongue as she departed at full speed. All in Middle English, naturally.

So, a few days later, there was a grand wedding feast with dozens of guests, music, dancing, food and wine.

Oh, that food. Oh, that wine. You never saw so much in all your life. People ate and drank till they fell down flat on the rushes – which were a clean spread for spring and the wedding feast.

But the castle servants and the villagers weren't happy. They feared Sir Antacill was there to stay, and Sir Oswald was looking very frail after this latest expedition, for he was really getting past galloping over the desert fighting the Saracens, who were rather better at it than he was.

Fat Johanna wasn't happy either though she organized all the feasting brilliantly. "What's up?" asked Mathilda as they snuggled under the old furs that night, and after Peredoc had licked them thoroughly, that being their goodnight wash. Sometimes he did Mathilda's teeth after she'd had a tasty supper. No, don't flinch. They just weren't squeamish. Why should you be?

"Ich crie vor min Dayesye," Johanna said, which meant she was worrying about her lamb, her Mathilda. And she was right to do so. Sir Antacill intended sorting out the estate, Castle Adamant and its inhabitants once he'd married Avelina, and the future looked very black for Mathilda.

Chapter Five

Jason, for once in his life, said nothing at all, just rolled up his eyes and keeled over on to Sam, who grabbed him in surprise but thrown off balance by the unexpected weight then staggered backwards into Chrystal Ewing, who shrieked very loudly and fell on to Hilary Jenkins standing just at the top of the stone spiral staircase, down which he descended which could have been very nasty, except that Phrynne Jamieson, who had a feeling that something strange was going on, had decided to do a bit of exploring on her own, and she managed to stop Hilary at the first bend, though not before he'd grazed his knee and banged his head. His cries and screams were alarming.

"I knew it. I knew there was something horrible. I knew there was something horrible," he cried over and over again as Mr Pridmore rushed to rescue him and Mrs Cooper hauled Jason to his feet, announcing with no sympathy whatsoever that that was the last time she was taking Jason anywhere.

"Do you mind?" shouted the curator. "May we have some order here? This is a Museum, remember."

You could hear the assistant curator muttering to himself: "I hate school parties. I knew there would be trouble the minute I laid eyes on this horrible bunch of kids."

"Let him have some air," sang out Mrs Cooper. "Children, clear a space. Jason, pull yourself together."

"I don't think he can. He's a very funny colour," put in Sam.

Reluctant as she was to admit that there might be something actually wrong with Jason, Mrs Cooper couldn't help but see that he was a very funny colour indeed, khaki possibly

"Something horrible. Oh, something horrible," wailed Hilary, from the arms of Mr Pridmore.

Alarm was starting to spread among other members of Class 4z, some of whom were genuinely scared, while others didn't mind adding a touch of drama to what was turning out to be a splendid outing.

"I think you'd better go," suggested the curator to Mrs Cooper, in a loud voice. "There are other schools here, you know, as well as yours."

"What about my History?" cried Mr Pridmore.

"When you've got a class in that state, it's best to leave History for the future," was the reply.

Mrs Cooper settled it all. "Class 4z," she said. "Outside. Quietly."

Thus it was that Jason came to in the alleyway in front of the Priory. The first thing he saw was Mrs Cooper. He'd never been fond of her, looking on her as something you had to put up with, like dentists, rainy days or greens, but when he saw her face, he cried: "Keep her away."

Mrs Cooper was not pleased. "If you think I have any wish to be holding you, you are quite wrong, Jason Bodger. And since you're obviously feeling better we'll see about getting back to school."

"Don't leave me," cried Jason, clutching her.

"Make up your mind," she said, detaching her silk blouse from some chewing gum sticking to Jason's grimy paw.

"Don't let her get me," moaned Jason.

"I think the sooner you get home and go to bed the better," decided Mrs Cooper. "Thank goodness it's Friday. I shall need the weekend to recover."

She thought longingly of her quiet bungalow, the smooth lawns, the bright flowers, its peace and tranquillity, Sebastian the Siamese cat, so elegant, so beautifully behaved, and her fat little husband, Hubert, so tubby, so gentle and courteous. Then with a deep sigh she set about organizing Mr Pridmore and thirty-two children (two of them acting very strangely) back to school.

Jason recovered over a weekend most of which was spent in wondering how he was to live down the shame of fainting and being seen clutching Mrs Cooper. Every time he thought about it he went hot all over. He'd have to do something, otherwise his position of Boss in Class 4z would be in danger.

The question was what?

But whenever he started to think up a plan something got in its way, came into his mind, something or rather someone—a girl with purple eyes, wearing a pudding cloth on her head, walking on air and holding out bony hands as she talked double Dutch to him. And when this happened Jason had to sit down and clutch his stomach which felt as though it had nose-dived into his boots.

On Sunday he didn't go out to play when his friends came to call. Instead he lay on his bed, feet on the pillow, while his poor brain churned and chugged away at his two problems: what to do to get back his macho image in the eyes of Class 4z, and how to blot out for ever the vision of the vanishing pudding-cloth girl in the Priory. Since he had no intention of setting foot in that place again for the rest of his life he wouldn't *see* her, so all he had to do was forget that dreadful school visit, and put it all out of his mind.

"Jason must be ill. He's been quiet all day," said his mother at the end of it.

"I hope he stays that way then. Best Sunday I've had in ages," said his sister.

"I do wonder if there's something the matter," his mother continued, for the most unlikely children have loving mothers.

"Course there isn't. What could be the matter? He's got no feelings to get hurt or anything like that and he's as tough as old boots."

And this conversation just shows how unfeeling people can be, and how it's possible to suffer alone.

By Monday morning he felt better. He went to school taking with him his new football and a new penknife, given to him by his uncle for a recent birthday, with eight blades and a special gadget for taking stones out of horses' hooves. That should be really useful, his uncle had said when he handed it over. Knives were forbidden in school so Jason thought it would polish up his image quite brightly if he flashed it around at play-time. And new footballs were always admired since the confiscation level was high.

Actually nothing went off quite as planned. He didn't have time to collect an admiring audience round the new knife, because the moment he arrived in the classroom, Mrs Cooper said, "And hand over that knife, Jason Bodger, before it causes some damage," though he could've sworn it wasn't showing at all. Sometimes he wondered if Mrs Cooper could possibly be a witch. She then departed, leaving Mr Pridmore in charge, so Jason managed to cause a fair amount of havoc. The class was divided into groups, with Mr Pridmore meaning to talk to each group in turn, but Jason's group orchestrated and conducted by Jason made so much noise and fuss that Mr Pridmore never got to the rest. Later when he was writing up his file about the day's activities, he looked down at the page and found he'd written, "There are times when I think that emptying dustbins would be a much pleasanter way of making a living," and had to paint it out with Tippex, before his tutor read it.

At play-time Jason, in high spirits, led the way outside with the new ball and a great game followed, Jason scoring all the goals in the lines painted on the wall for that purpose. As the whistle blew at the end of play Jason kicked the ball straight at the one window not protected from breakage by wire mesh, the cloakroom window, and smash it went, glass splintering everywhere, glittering in the sunlight.

Mr Pridmore, learning all about the joy of playground duty, sent him to the Headmaster, where Jason remained for the rest of the morning, so that Mr Pridmore was able to take quite a successful and orderly Maths lesson, which made him feel better, while the Headmaster reduced Jason to a tiny worm. However, when he finally got back to his class he managed to swagger and show off again and impress the kids by his account of just what he'd said to the Headmaster (which actually was nothing at all). As he ate his lunch and half Hilary Jenkins's, Jason thought life was fine and last Friday's visit was just something to be forgotten. In the afternoon it was to be P.E. Jason liked P.E. He was good at it, especially on the ropes and beams . . . no, something said in his head, don't think about beams . . . that was last Friday and Friday was a day now gone for ever like that vanishing girl.

Right now everything was fine . . .

Jason Bodger rules OK?

Chapter Six

The honeymoon (or whatever they had in those days) of Antacill and Avelina was short. To begin with they mainly threw things at each other, until, finally exhausted, they sat down and began to talk, finding out as they did so that they wanted the same things from life: to be richer than anyone else, to be more powerful than anyone else, and to be more admired than anyone else. Getting down to the nitty-gritty they wanted to get rid of Oswald and all the girls, kill Fat Johanna and Max and put down the villagers who'd grown far too democratic and uppity under Sir Oswald, then build up a super fighting force led by Terrible Tirrell and his band of cutthroats, to attack, pillage and plunder as many castles in the kingdom as possible, grabbing all their wealth and armouries. Antacill also fancied a captured maiden or so, but he didn't tell Avelina that.

"Where do I begin?" he crooned in her ear, thinking that she wasn't as hideous as he'd first thought, though he still intended to push her quietly down a well when he'd really established himself as Lord of the Manor, and find himself a beauty. But she'd got a good brain and he might as well make use of her for as long as he could stand it or her.

"Get rid of Father first. Poison would do."

"Not with Fat Johanna there it won't. And remember nothing's to happen to her till another one's trained to draw (the fire) and (work the) spit."

"Let's have a hunt. Then he can be accidentally killed," she suggested.

"We had a lot of hunting before you and I were wed," he replied, kissing her hand.

"But not boar-hunting. Not dangerous stuff," she murmured, nibbling his ear.

"There don't appear to be any boars in the forest at the moment," said Anck.

"There must be. They need stirring up. Send out Tirrell. He'd stir anything up. And get him to go round the villagers while he's about it and bring them to their knees with new taxes and more work on our land so they can't do any of their own."

You can see Avelina was almost as nasty as Antacill.

"Great." Please remember that this conversation was taking place in Middle English.

"Can I come with you to the hunt where Dad gets knocked off?"

This shocked even Antacill. "Not very womanly, my dear, is it?"

"Sucks to being womanly. I want some fun."

During the following week one of the village children spotted a ferocious beast in the forest and returned home babbling of tusks as long and sharp as spears. Next day another fierce wild pig, goaded on by Tirrell and his mates, rushed squealing and yelping right through the centre of the wattle and daubs, knocking a couple of wives out of the way, which as they grumbled later is not what you want at all when you're out gathering herbs and veg. for the evening meal. Something had to be done. The villagers complained to Max, who went to Sir Oswald, who said ask Antacill. He really was getting past it, I'm afraid.

So it was that the cry went up of Tally ho, the boar, the boar, and lots of men went around boasting of what they'd done last time there was a boar-hunt.

Max, who had actually killed the boar, being severely gashed for his trouble, felt most depressed. He hated boar-hunts. Someone always got hurt, crops were wrecked and work neglected, and Max liked life to be an orderly routine, growing and making things, improving everything generally. Fat Johanna, of course, knew something was *up*, so she sent Jos and Mathilda spying and they soon found out that Tirrell and his mates were driving a boar colony towards the village from the other side of the wooded hills several miles distant.

A hunt was fixed, although winter not spring was the true hunting season. Max was the leader, Tirrell second in command, with Sir Oswald officially directing it, which meant nothing at all since he was going a bit gaga. Every man and boy was to take part, while the women and girls were to stay behind and prepare a feast for the victorious menfolk, organized by Fat Johanna who though she resented the fact that the men had all the flash and showing-off part, did herself feel that cooking some good grub in the kitchen was more enjoyable than crawling round in the forest undergrowth after an ill-tempered and dangerous animal.

In the end Avelina did not go. Boar-hunts are not at all like hunting deer or foxes or hares or otters: you can get killed, and by now she was expecting a Little Anckie, and hoping that it would be a *boy*. Antacil was as pleased as punch about this and thought that if she managed a son then he might keep her after all, instead of pushing her down a well. So only one female attended the hunt, and you can guess who that was, our Mathilda, dressed up in Jos's old clothes with Peredoc at her side. Fat Johanna kissed and hugged her and Jos and told them to look after Sir Oswald. She told nearly everyone else the same.

Into the wild forest the hunt set off with horses and hounds, though not many horses since most people were on foot, with a motley collection of hounds, belling and calling, indeed a terrible noise with avoy, avoy, Tally ho, tilly ho, avaunt, shelloh, haloh, arere, gobble, gobble, way hey there, swef, swef and so on, people falling over one another, and all of them telling someone else what to do. Weapons here, there and everywhere, Jos noting them, what they were, and who'd got what, spears and boar-spears, swords, daggers and falchions, knives, crossbows and longbows, cudgels, sharpened sticks and rounded stones. Horns rang and sang, the stirrup cup was passed round and they were off. By this time most animals were disappearing fast to another part of the forest, anxious to escape from such a rabble.

In the centre of it all rode Sir Oswald, vague and slightly bonkers, and Sir Antacill, evil and nasty.

At first Mathilda was not scared. Partly because it was not her nature, and partly because she was concentrating on not being recognized, lest she be sent back. She'd even smeared soot on Peredoc to make him a different colour. But she needn't have worried. Everyone was so busy milling about in the undergrowth they didn't notice her small scruffy figure. All her thoughts were fixed on Sir Oswald and that she must be ready to save him when necessary, not that he'd ever done a thing for her but she didn't want him finished off by 'orrible Anck. She didn't really think about the boar at all.

The hordes of people thinned out as some got stuck and others fell behind. Jos and Mathilda kept ahead for they knew all the ways of the forest and they were little and good at scrambling through tricky places. After an hour or so, Sir Oswald, Sir Antacill, Max, the foresters, some villagers and the soldiers arrived at a clearing, hard behind the hounds singing into the afternoon.

And there was the boar. On the other side of the clearing. Just like that.

Bristly and fierce and angry and bloodstained – two of the dogs were dead – and tusky and frightening and explosive and terrifying and sad as all hunted things are, sad with piggy red eyes, bloody tusks, mad with rage, a wild thing. Peredoc whiffled through his nose and tried to get at him. Mathilda strained to hold him to her. For at last she was afraid. There was the boar, the quarry, a beast at bay, a beast that could kill, could kill *her, her, Mathilda.*

He seemed about to charge. Max and his men knelt

holding their boar-spears, which had a cross-bar on them to hold off the hurtling boar while the point of the spear did its deadly work. The hounds bayed, the horns blew. And the boar charged straight at Max,

tusks covered with blood and foam and spit. Men retreated, but not Max, steady as a rock, crouched on the ground, with Jos suddenly beside him. Max motioned angrily for Jos to go, but he would not. He squatted beside his father, Max with his boar-spear, Jos with one of his many knives.

Tirrell fitted an arrow into his bow that seemed aimed at the boar but was intended to swivel towards Sir Oswald. His servants moved around him to protect him, but quicker than anyone, our Mathilda leapt forward and pushed Sir Oswald off his horse, just as the raving boar, already wearing two or three knives and swords among his bristles, leapt on Max, who held him on his boar-spear. Quick as a flash, Jos stabbed the animal to the middle, with his knife.

All was chaos, pandemonium. No one had a clue what was going on. But as people fell back, it could be seen that the boar was dead, Max and Jos were smiling shakily at each other, Sir Oswald was hanging half-way off his horse, very undignified, and Peredoc, swollen into an enormous dog, hairs a-bristle, hackles down his back, jaws and teeth wide, tail like a banner, growling deep inside his throat, was keeping the restive horses at bay as he stood over Mathilda lying white and still on the ground, Jos's cap knocked off, her flaming fleece of hair spread everywhere. And gazing at Mathilda, eyes full of questions, was Antacill.

Chapter Seven

Mrs Cooper was marking the register when Mr Pridmore's tutor, Mr Porter, put his head round the classroom door.

"No, don't get up, children," he boomed. He was a big, booming, bearded man. "I've come to watch your P.E. lesson. We'll have some fun."

"Fun? Fun? I'd rather go to the dentist for fun," Mr Pridmore thought wildly, wondering if he had the courage to run out of the room and go home, but he hadn't. He stood there and smiled instead.

"I'm sorry but I have to see the Head. I'll be as quick as I can," explained Mrs Cooper. "So I'll leave you for now."

"No, don't leave me," cried Mr Pridmore inside. "Please don't leave me with him, P.E. and Jason Bodger." For although he didn't like Mrs Cooper, there was that about her which made him feel safe. But he smiled bravely and murmured, "Yes, of course, Mrs Cooper."

Along the corridors and down the steps they went to the hall. Jason managed to trip up Hilary so that he fell down the steps and cried, but the tutor was reading

Mr Pridmore's teaching file and didn't see. On entering the hall Mr Pridmore couldn't see either. There had been a film-showing in the dinner hour and the heavy curtains were still blacking out the windows.

"Oh, no," thought Mr Pridmore. "We shall have to put out the apparatus," a job he dreaded. Fortunately the children had already changed into their P.E. kit. Out loud he said brightly: "Find a space and sit down in it till I've drawn back the curtains."

"Can't we have it in the dark?" asked Jason, but Mr Pridmore ignored this, pulling aside the curtains one by one and flooding the hall with light, then stepping backwards and falling over Chrystal Ewing, who had naturally chosen the wrong space to sit down in. Caught off balance, Mr Pridmore turned a backwards somersault to topple sprawling over Hilary, who was squashed beneath Mr Pridmore's six feet two inches. A loud wailing noise arose from Hilary and from Chrystal, but this was lost in hoots of laughter and the offers of help coming from the rest of the class.

"You need a white stick, Sir," roared Jason and was immediately told off by Phrynne for being so insensitive. After five minutes or so –

"Shall we go on with the lesson?" boomed the tutor.

"You wanted some fun, Sir," said Jason, quick as a flash.

Mr Pridmore elected four reliable children to unbolt the P.E. apparatus from the wall and swing it into position against the wall bars, thus bringing into play ropes, beam, trapeze, ladder and slide. Tricky it was, and easy to go wrong, so he didn't pick Jason but told him and Sam and two girls to put down mats, the box, balancing forms etc. instead. However, Phrynne, one of those chosen to fix the apparatus, was for once having difficulty pushing in the bolt, and Jason, having arranged the mats and the horse, noticed this and rushed across, full of glee, to show her how. Crossly, she went to push him away, the bolt pulled out and the whole apparatus swung loosely into the middle of the hall, out of control.

"Look out," shouted the tutor, on super boom, this time.

"Here," cried Mr Pridmore, tripping over Hilary Jenkins as he rushed towards the whole wobbly structure.

"I'm fixing it," shouted Jason, leaping up and grabbing the beam.

The two upright posts which needed to be bolted into the hall floor swayed alarmingly, as did the ropes, trapeze, ladder and slide, all swinging into position but not fixed. Chrystal Ewing shrieked and Hilary crouched on the mat hiding his head.

"I'm holding it steady," cried Jason, sailing through the air like a captain on a sinking ship in a hurricane. "Grab the posts . . . oh . . . oh . . ."

Swinging towards him from the other end of the beam like a Tarzaness flew the girl, black robe and head-cloth sailing behind her, purple eyes glittering, extraordinary sandalled feet waving in the air, one bony hand clutching the beam, the other reaching out eagerly to Jason. She was talking nineteen to the dozen. To Jason's terrified ears the words seemed to be double double Dutch. With a cry that wouldn't come properly out of his throat he dropped down off the beam, with only one wish – to escape from that hall as quickly as possible. And fell on to the humped form of Hilary who burst into tears.

"Just what is going on here?" Mrs Cooper spoke from the doorway. "Have you all gone mad? Mr Pridmore! Mr Porter! Jason Bodger, I might have known. Frynay, grab that post."

She had clicked across the hall and was already bolting down the other one. Jason lifted his eyes, where he had buried them in Hilary's tee shirt. For a moment all was still and in that quiet space Jason and the girl looked at each other, she said something to him and was gone.

"There was something, something here, Mrs Cooper. Honestly," said Phrynne. "I know there was."

"Horrible," wailed Hilary.

Mrs Cooper was not interested.

"Into your groups. Greens to the wall bars, reds to the forms, yellows to the springboard and box, blues to the ropes. Stand there till I give the word. Jason, Hilary, go and change, then sit down. Mr Porter, I'm sure you have other schools to visit. Mr Pridmore, we'll have a little talk later. Just now, please continue with your lesson."

And Mr Pridmore did.

Mrs Cooper moved over to Jason and Hilary.

"Just stop crying, Hilary. Everything will be all right. Try not to make such a fuss at every little thing. You can't go through life wrapped in cotton wool."

Hilary sniffed and subsided, wishing he could.

"Jason, what is it?"

"Miss . . . Mrs Cooper . . . I think . . . I think I'm seeing a . . . a . . . gh . . . ghost."

"Nonsense," she answered. "Probably indigestion. What you need is plenty of work. Bring me your Maths book and I'll set you some problems."

"I've got all the problems I need," murmured Jason, trailing away to the classroom in deep despair.

Chapter Eight

Back at the castle Mathilda soon recovered under the loving care of Fat Johanna. Max had settled Sir Oswald on his horse the right way up, and Segg carried Mathilda home in his arms with no effort whatsoever, as he was built like Tarzan except for his short legs. Besides, Jos and Segg were the only two that Peredoc would allow near Mathilda, so Jos took the dog and Segg, Mathilda. Max just managed to stop Tirrell shooting Peredoc. The boar was carried aloft in triumph, plus any other game captured while they were hunting and I won't go into details as I know you all get easily upset. I'll just say that the castle and the village were well stocked for some time. Just like a really big visit to the supermarket, in fact. Fat Johanna was delighted with it all, and also pleased to find Sir Oswald still alive if not exactly kicking. She cried a little over her Dayesye who had been knocked down by Sir Oswald's horse, a rather stupid animal, but her Dayesye was a strong girl and soon recovered, especially with all the special rubbing lotions and potions and broths and so on, given to her by Fat Johanna, who saved Mathilda the best of everything going.

But the damage was done. Sir Antacill had spotted her. Up till then he'd hardly been aware of her existence. But now he was. He enquired all about her from Avelina, who described her as a murdering serpent – except for Eleanor, the sisters had always insisted that Mathilda 'murdered' their mother – and a loathsome spy. Sir Antacill thought about Mathilda at some length, how she'd managed to foil Tirrell's effort to finish off Sir Os, and he remembered her strawberry-blonde hair and deep blue eyes and – I bet this surprises you – her beauty. Yes, dirty legs, ghastly manners, the lot, Mathilda was the best-looking girl in the forest, though still very young of course. What's more, she had something which nobody else in her family had – except perhaps Avelina and in her case it had all turned sour early in life – brains and character. But much more than that, Mathilda was the kind of person people follow to the ends of the earth, struggling through deserts and jungles although they hate travel, climbing mountains though they're scared of heights, crossing oceans though they're always sea-sick. Yes, she of the dirty legs and rotten manners was one of those. Boudicca was another. You can probably think of some more yourself. Jolly uncomfortable they often are. Fat Johanna knew this, as did Jos and Max and Segg and the villagers and the castle servants. Sir Oswald and his family didn't but then they were silly, stupid people. Jason Bodger was slowly realizing it, and Sir Antacill knew quality when he saw it.

She was going to be trouble, this one.

She must be got rid of.

Avelina was thrilled at the idea. "What I've always wanted," she cried. "Drop her in a well."

Sir Antacill looked at her sharply. Was she a mind-reader, by any chance? She'd been looking so unlovely lately he'd more than once thought of wells.

"No, her death would cause trouble. Besides . . ."

"Besides what, Anckie darling?"

Please don't forget that all this is in Middle English.

"Humph," said Anckie darling, who'd just been about to say that besides it'd be a pity to murder such a smasher, but hastily decided against it. "I've got work to do, dearest."

And he wandered off, leaving Avelina to think of the castle without Mathilda. He himself was thinking that Mathilda was really going to be a bit of all right quite soon, and if she married him, he'd have no trouble at all in ruling the castle, followed by more castles, followed by . . . why not . . . the country? Why not, indeed? King Antacill? Queen Mathilda? What's more, her deep, deep blue eyes and pretty nose and wonderful hair would be there right beside him instead of . . . awful Avelina.

But he had to keep Avelina happy till she had a son, and if she didn't, well, **WELL** would be the answer. And he had to keep Mathilda hidden in case anyone else spotted and snatched her up. Why, if she weren't properly guarded any visiting lord or minstrel . . . or page or peasant . . . or any one, perhaps even that boy Joe, son of boring, beastly, loyal Max, could run off with her, the mind boggled! No, she must be stowed away somewhere safe for a while until he could safely get *his* hands on her, for the more he thought about it, the more sure he grew that he wanted her, not Avelina. No problem, it could be easily and quietly done. But if she was to be his future wife she'd need a bit of polish, some education. He could see she was very wild at the moment, chasing after boar-hunts in boy's clothes, all that would have to stop. She'd need to learn to sing and play the lute and how to embroider and how to tell the servants what to do, woman's stuff. Then when she was a suitable age, thirteen or fourteen, he'd marry her. All settled.

"Bring me Fat Johanna," he said to his page. "I want to have some discourse with her."

You'd never have guessed from the way she stood there, fine big handsome woman that she was, though now of course very old, by their standards, how terrified Fat Johanna was and how wildly her heart was pounding. She knew trouble lay ahead. The signs had been bad all week, comets in the heavens and a frog croaking on the bed, a magpie walking up and down on the highest tower. Gloom and doom all the way.

She curtsied, as little as possible.

"Prepare the Lady Mathilda for a journey."

"What journey, may I ask, sir?"

"To receive education at a certain Priory. That is all you need to know at present. I'm sure you will rejoice in her good fortune."

"But she is already educated."

"Oh?"

"My father was learned. He taught me to read and to write and to count. And so I taught Mathilda."

"How?"

"I taught her with everything about us, in the kitchen, in the castle, in the forest. And my father gave me a little book he owned . . ."

The moment she spoke she regretted it. Books were so rare that they were like gold dust.

"Bring it to me."

"But it's mine!"

"Don't argue. It's mine *now*. I can't have a stupid woman cook owning a book!"

Fat Johanna changed her tactics.

"Does Sir Oswald know you're sending Mathilda away?"

"The Lady Mathilda to you. You know as well as I do that where she's concerned he doesn't want to know."

"Must she go?" asked Fat Johanna and again wished she hadn't. Taking away happiness was one of Antacill's hobbies.

"Just get her ready. And the other one, what's her name? The batty one, you know the one I mean."

"Julietta?"

"Yes, she can be company for Mathilda. And Bertha or whatever her name is. That's two more dowries we shan't have to hand over."

"You have to send something with girls going into a priory or nunnery."

"There's bound to be rubbish lying around the castle that'll do. Or they might have a bit of jewellery tucked away. Organize it, woman."

"Yes, Sir," said Fat Johanna softly, screaming inside.

Bright moonlight in the forest, white on the paths and in the clearings, black in the shadows of trees. Fat Johanna on one horse, Jos and Mathilda on another were making an escape, accompanied by Segg who was to see them safely (they hoped) to the edge of the Chetwynde lands. Max had found them the horses, Fat Johanna the provisions, and Peredoc easily kept up with them, very easily, for they were going too slowly, as Segg and Fat Johanna knew. Segg was to return to the castle, while they went on to Wales and the castle of Robyn and Eleanor, where they hoped to find safety and time for Mathilda and Jos to grow up and defeat Sir Antacill and Avelina.

Mathilda and Jos were excited at such an adventure, for Jos having little imagination had few fears, while Mathilda with an imagination as huge as the universe always believed she'd come out on top. On they travelled through the night and the news of the flight was passed from owl to fox to badger and so on along the line all the way to Wales.

But Fat Johanna was dead miserable. She missed her bed and comfortable routine, and besides she was afraid they weren't going to get away with it. Perhaps they should have allowed Mathilda to leave for the convent and while she was growing up there in safety, use the time to gather allies for the day when they could strike back at the revolting Antacill and the hateful Avelina. And, honestly, kids, this would have been the best plan, but when Mathilda was told the news, she cried and wanted to run away, and when her Dayesye cried, Fat Johanna went bananas, losing all her usual common sense. And so off they set on this

mad escape project. Riding through the dark shadows of the trees terrified Fat Johanna, for the eeriness of that vast and lonely place at night was to her almost unbearable. She feared the forest. She was a very civilized person. She liked people and chat and things going on all around her.

What am I saying? Things going on all around her? There were. Segg paused and listened, and a low growling noise set up in Perêdoc's throat.

"We're being followed," he whispered. "Hide and let them go past."

Silently they slithered into a dark clump of bushes and trees, holding the horses and the dog as still as possible while the chink of hooves and jangle of harness sounded too close for comfort, right beside them. A man's voice, sounding like Tirrell's, swore, and a string of soldiers rode past, unaware of their quarry so close to the forest ride.

"Now," whispered Segg when all the sounds had died away. Cautiously they emerged and clambered back on to the horses, and once more rode into the night.

Dawn was breaking pink and pearly over the now much nearer hills as Segg stopped at the edge of the Chetwynde terrain. He raised a hand to salute Mathilda, turned to go, then cried out a warning that was chopped in half. So was Peredoc's snarl as a blackness much deeper than that of the forest fell upon them. Tirrell and his Beastly Band had arrived.

Chapter Nine

The next time Mathilda's ghost appeared was in a large store*, one of those selling everything from underwear to food. Jason was out shopping with his mother at the time, very reluctantly for he had to have a new pair of school trousers his mother said, his old ones were indecent.

Some days earlier Jason wouldn't have argued much for he didn't seem to have his old powers any more. Some fire, some spark had left him. He no longer got up in the morning ready to attack life, to try out new tricks, new schemes, new games. Instead he lay, head under the bedclothes, thinking, however much he tried to push her out of his mind, of a girl on a beam, visible or invisible, a girl with purple eyes and a cloth on her head, a very thin girl, talking to him in double Dutch, asking him for something, beseeching him . . . Jason Bodger would then get up and refuse his breakfast. He didn't fancy his grub any more. So he grew thinner and taller and quieter and dreamier. Sam Stokes found another friend. Hilary Jenkins found he

*I'm not allowed to tell you its name.

was no longer tormented and so grew bossy and objectionable himself: Hilary Jenkinses always do. Mr Pridmore congratulated himself on getting on top of his work and the class at last. Mrs Cooper said nothing but had a chat with Mrs Bodger after school. They agreed on extra vitamins and cod-liver oil. Jason's class thought he'd either gone soft or barmy. But they didn't dare say so in his hearing because he was still the biggest kid in Class 4z, even if newly wet.

Phrynne Jamieson came over to him in the dinner hour where he brooded on a bank, watching cricket instead of organizing it as he would once have done, and sat down beside him.

"I think she lived there, you know," she said after a bit.

Jason took no notice.

"At the Priory."

Jason turned away. He didn't want to listen to clever stuck-up Phrynne Jamieson. What could she have to say that could possibly be interesting?

"I asked my mother to get me a book about the Priory and about the nuns who lived there. It was a nun you saw, wasn't it?"

He was interested now all right. Rigid all over, robot man, he managed to nod his head stiffly up and down, face still turned away from Phrynne.

"I sort of saw her, you know. Oh, not like you, but very faintly, like a pale shadow moving . . ."

"Oh, yes, she moves all right," Jason said at last. "A right mover, she is."

"She was a young one, wasn't she?"

Jason managed to nod. "Is," he muttered.

"Sometimes they took them young. Sometimes they were unhappy . . ."

"I don't want to know." Jason stood up. "I don't want to think about it. I don't want to talk to you. Go away. Push off, Phrynne Jamieson. There wasn't anything. Nothing at all. I'm off to play cricket. Get lost."

And he rushed away to join in the game, which he played very badly.

"I'm sorry but I don't think you'll be in the team this year, Jason, unless you buck up a bit," said Mrs Cooper.

"I don't care," thought Jason and mooched off to the far end of the field and threw himself down under some trees. "I don't care about anything." And he put his head down on his knees in despair from finding out that he, Jason Bodger, the toughest, most macho boy in school, didn't care about anything but just wanted to sit and bawl like some wet girl, some unhappy wet girl, some unhappy ghost of a girl but not wet at all, brave and with something badly wrong that she kept trying to tell him. He got up and ran three times right round the field to get away from her and from himself and collapsed pale, shattered and knackered, a ghost of himself. Phrynne Jamieson was waiting for him.

"Actually the best information was in a very old book my mother got out of the Cathedral library, at least she read it in there for you can't remove the books. They unlocked the cupboard it was in. She was interested in what I told her about you and she wanted to find out more about the Priory. She's a History teacher."

"I know. She teaches my sister. Get lost, Phrynne Jamieson."

"You can tell me to get lost, Jason, but you can't tell her, that ghost, can you? She'll be back to fetch you. You wait and see."

That night Jason hardly slept at all. He lay waiting for the ghost to appear at the foot of the bed with beckoning finger. At last he couldn't bear it, switched his light on, put his head under the pillow and, round about four o'clock, finally fell asleep. Next morning his mother began to tell him off for leaving his light on, but stopped when she saw his sad, pale face with the dark rings under his eyes.

"Go back to bed. I'm phoning the doctor."

"I think Jason's got a mystery illness," she said to his sister, as Jason crawled thankfully back to bed.

"Rubbish," his sister answered. "Mum, Mrs Jamieson's going to take us on a tour of the old Priory in town. That'll be great, won't it?"

"I don't know," her mother replied, wondering. "I've just realized. It's since Jason went there that he's been so peculiar."

"Improved, I'd say. I can do my homework in peace, these days. See you, Mum, 'bye."

Mrs Bodger went up the stairs intent on asking Jason just what had happened on that visit that changed him so, but he was already asleep, and she then had to ring the doctor and make arrangements about her own job. But as she did so she kept wondering, had he picked up some rare virus from those old Priory walls? Was it lurking there through the centuries, waiting to attack Jason? Nonsense, I'll make a cup of coffee, she told herself.

The doctor said there was nothing wrong with Jason

but he was a little run down, and prescribed some tablets and recommended a short holiday. Mrs Bodger rang up her sister in Cornwall, and Jason was despatched there despite his uncle saying that no, on no account was he having that frightful child in the house again, he remembered his last visit, in fact he would never forget it. Jason's holiday there is not part of this story, but he had a smashing time, fought his cousins, nearly got drowned, fell down part of a cliff and wrecked a tractor. He returned to home and school, tanned and fit and horrible, and if anyone had mentioned ghosts to him he would have shouted a rude word, meaning rubbish. His uncle, on the other hand, had to visit *his* doctor, where he was told that he needed a holiday.

Back at school Jason was his old self again. He ignored Phrynne, reduced Hilary to tears, and decided to help Mr Pridmore with his teaching, proving so successful that when Mr Pridmore came to write up his file that night, all he could manage was "Jason Bodger is back!" His room mate found him there later fast asleep, head on the file. Worn out, poor thing, he thought and went off to a party. He had a very nice class for teaching practice and wanted to stay with them for always.

It was on the following Saturday morning that Mrs Bodger said Jason had to have new trousers for school. Had it or they been jeans Jason would have taken an interest, but school trousers are among the boring things in life. Still, he had no choice and off he went to the big store, quite near the Priory, not that Jason thought of that. Priories and ghosts were never in his mind these days. If he thought of them at all he put it down to the mystery illness, that his mother, at least, believed in. The word 'beam' could make him twitch a bit, though. But as he stood there, bored out of his tiny mind with the purchasing of school trousers, "beams" didn't mean a thing.

"I just want to get a few things for the weekend," said his mother, heading for the food department. Collecting a basket, she bought some salad stuff, nearly as boring as school trousers for Jason liked junk food.

"Now I want a cooked chicken. We're nearly finished, Jason, and you've been very good, for once."

The refrigerated counter was covered in roast chickens. Mrs Bodger selected one. Jason yawned.

And right in the middle of that counter appeared the girl, perched on several carcasses, her mouth wide open to speak to Jason.

"Ich . . ." she began, then her purple eyes flashed and she seized a whole chicken and began to eat, stuffing it down her open mouth as fast as she could. Jason, turned to stone, knew that he'd known she was very hungry, almost starving. Somewhere, someone began to scream on a repetitive high note.

"He's stolen a chicken . . ."

"A chicken's disappeared . . ."

"Jason, what's going on? What are you doing?" That was Mrs Bodger.

Statue Jason didn't know what anyone was seeing. He could see his girl; yes, he knew she was his girl now, there was no getting away from it. The love in her eyes was more than he could bear and it wasn't something he could escape from. And there she sat, thin as a rail, stuffing herself with food as fast as poss., only pausing once to grin at him.

"Fetch the assistant."

"Fetch the manager."

"Fetch the store detective."

"Fetch the police."

"Stop that woman screaming."

"Catch the child's mother. She's going to faint."

"That's 'cos she took it."

"No, it was the boy."

"Where is it now?"

The girl had finished the chicken. She threw the bones over the back of the counter and smiled at Jason, and then she spotted the cakes, jellies and trifles on the next counter. With a cry and a bound she was upon them.

"Look, look, look. That cake's disappearing now!"

"It can't be that pair then, they're over there."

"But they're responsible."

"Jason, just let's go," moaned his mother. Out-of-action robot Jason couldn't move. Where the girl was, he had to be.

"Now, now, just what's going on here?" asked a familiar-sounding voice. The law had arrived.

But so had Phrynne. And her mother.

Phrynne's clear up-market snobby voice that Jason had always hated was speaking. "I think we can help."

Her mother was saying, "I can vouch for Mrs Bodger."

And the girl, shaking back her head-cloth, and standing up, one foot on an apple tart and the other on a box of éclairs, seized a particularly rich Black Forest gateau, blew a kiss at Jason, put her tongue out at Phrynne and disappeared. So did the gateau.

"I'm the manager. I suggest we all go into my office," said a voice, and Jason found he could move again.

Chapter Ten

And so Mathilda arrived at last (and so have we) in front of that small, square, red sandstone building with the big chimneys that Jason, eight hundred years later, will think looks like an old barn; St Katherine's Priory. I bet he wouldn't have known it *then* though, mint new, standing in a flowery meadow with the Mynchon stream flowing through it, not a shop nor pavement in sight. Mr Pridmore and Phrynne will think they know what a Day in the Life of a Nun in the Middle Ages would be like, but they will only guess from books. Mathilda was about to learn what it was really all about, as Tirrell banged on the huge door, bonk, bonk, bonk, while Bertha, Julietta, and the soldiers waited to be let in, all of them dirty, hungry and tired.

For what a journey they'd had, through miles of forests, across streams and rivers, up valleys, and down hills, at one time following through the levels and swamps the old, old road, perhaps the oldest in the country (wicker mats laid on mud). And except for worrying about Fat Johanna, Jos and Peredoc, and wondering what had happened to them after they'd been captured (for Mathilda was whisked away and sent off to the Priory immediately) she loved every minute of it. Oh, yes, she wanted to escape from Tirrell, and tried to on more than one occasion but they always brought her back, and in the end she gave up and enjoyed this whole new world that she hadn't realized was so big and beautiful. She felt she'd like to travel for ever, perhaps go on a Crusade like her father, after she'd driven Antacill out of the Castle, of course. But sometimes at night when they lay down to sleep in some old barn or under the stars, she thought of Peredoc licking between her toes and cried herself to sleep.

At last they arrived at the Priory and Tirrell smote with his great fist.

The heavy door opened and a nun stood there.

"Christianna," cried Bertha, throwing her arms round her, followed by Julietta who always copied what others did in the hope of getting things right, poor lamb. After embracing them this nun turned to Mathilda, smiling a thin smile as if it hurt. "I've been told by our dear sister Avelina and the noble Lord Antacill, her husband, to take special care of you."

Mathilda's heart sank. Sister Christianna looked just like Avelina, and though she'd left the Castle a long time ago, Mathilda could remember being whipped by her, though it might have been Avelina. She pushed the thought out of her mind as Sister Christianna drew forward another nun, this time the spitting image of Tirrell, no, it can't be possible, thought Mathilda, not two of them!

But Sister Christianna was speaking.

"You will be in Sister Hilda's special charge, Mathilda, and you must obey her in all things for your spiritual welfare."

Not on your nelly, thought Mathilda in Middle English as Sister Hilda nodded to her and then spoke to Tirrell –

"Greetings, brother," which solved that one for Mathilda. Tired and hungry as she was she found their unfriendly faces just too much, and wanted to crawl into a dark hole and not come out for a long time. But then a little old nun, knee high to a grasshopper, with quick bright eyes, pushed through the two tall sisters and smiled so warmly at Mathilda that she couldn't believe it.

"Sister Superior says that the young novices are to be bathed and fed and rested, and the soldiers are to go to their quarters where they will be given food and ale."

Sister Christianna frowned at the little nun, who grinned back at her, and beckoned the three girls to follow her, which they did thankfully. And so at last Mathilda entered the Priory, stepping into that square hall with fat pillars. It was cool and clean.

"Follow me," said the little nun and down a winding staircase they went. "I'm Sister Theresa," she told them, "and I'm second only to Sister Superior, though it's sometimes difficult to get Sister Christianna to remember this. Here we are."

The room was small and very bare though Mathilda didn't notice. Her eyes were fixed on a tub of water, warm and welcoming. Now Mathilda had only ever bathed in the moat and the river. Imagine!!! She stared in wonder, Bertha and Julietta as well, while Sister Theresa laughed at them. And Sister Christianna and Sister Hilda appeared – terrified that they might miss something.

Their clothes were taken away and they were put into shifts rather like nightgowns and in these they had to take their baths because it was thought immodest to bathe with nothing on, which astonished Mathilda who'd done it hundreds of times in the moat and the river at home. She would, of course. Still, she felt marvellous afterwards (you try waiting for a long time, a very long time, and see how you feel when you finally get a bath, no, on second thoughts, don't). Her hair was washed so that it flowed out all round her in a great mane of crinkles and curly bits. She hoped they wouldn't shave it off. She'd heard in the castle that that was what they did to nuns, and Sister Hilda did indeed appear with her shears and cropped off Bertha's mousey locks and Julietta's wisps. Julietta screamed, poor lamb, at the sight of the shears, and Mathilda muttered, "Go easy on her," to Hilda, and had her mane tugged sharply. Mathilda waited for her turn, but nothing happened. Her hair was left long, though tied back and bundled up. Then they were given their clothes, called habits. Scratchy they were, and Mathilda's hair was concealed under what Jason would think of later as her pudding cloth, and, last of all, they were given a long string of beads to tie at their waists.

"For your prayers," said Sister Hilda, giving Mathilda a sharp nudge.

"Now I shall take you to the Refectory for some food," smiled Sister Theresa.

"Thank goodness for that. I'm starving," thought Mathilda as they trotted along towards the stairway again. But Fat Johanna was not cook here, and all they received was some very thin soup and some very hard bread. Still, they soon ate it all up.

"Now you shall meet Sister Superior," said Sister Theresa at last, and led them along a corridor and up another winding staircase into a small bare room where a very old woman lay on a narrow pallet. The girls knelt down and she opened her eyes and smiled. Then she stretched out a hand and laid it on each head in turn, and closed her eyes again. Sister Theresa beckoned them to come away.

They were then taken to a small chapel and told to pray and meditate. So Mathilda did. She meditated on her situation and what she was going to do about it. Her general aim was clear. She was going to escape and raise an army to free the castle from Antacill and reinstate Sir Oswald, with Max and Fat Johanna advising him till she, Mathilda, was old enough to do it all herself, female or not, blowed to that. Her plan was fine. What she needed to fill in were the details.

Some weeks later it seemed to Mathilda that she'd lived in the Priory for ever. A Day in the Life of Mathilda the Novice was like a year. She'd always known freedom, had taken it for granted, roaming through the castle and the countryside just as she pleased, coming and going without questionings, for Fat Johanna never nagged but always welcomed. With Jos and Peredoc and Fat Johanna to love her and teach her she didn't miss a thing——

Until now, when she missed it all, the kitchen, the grub, the castle, the chit-chat, the woods and the animals, the moat and the river. As she lay on the thin hard bed in the dorter, with its scratchy blanket that wasn't warm enough, and Sister Hilda continually coming over to cross her arms forcibly across her chest, for that was how they had to lie, memories of the fur-laden bed, with that best of furs, Peredoc, licking between her toes, would come strongly to her and tears would gush and she'd uncross her arms to wipe them away and Sister Hilda would rush over and bang them together again . . . and so on. Sister Hilda was built like her brother Tirrell so Mathilda's arms were covered with bruises. Eventually she stopped thinking about them all for it always made her cry, and besides she feared they were dead or in prison, leaving no one left to care about, though she quite liked some of the nuns, especially Sister Theresa, and had grown quite fond of barmy Julietta. But Sister Theresa and Julietta could not replace Fat Johanna and Jos.

Worst of all she was always being woken up. All of the time. So she was tired as well as bored.

Mathilda's Day in the Life of . . . went like this.

Bed at seven.

Prayers at midnight.

Prayers at one o'clock.

More prayers at half past five.

Breakfast, goody, at six-thirty followed by reading and prayers until nine o'clock when they were allowed to talk to each other. In Latin, of course, and though

Mathilda had learned some with Fat Johanna it wasn't exactly a lively chat time.

Ten o'clock was High Mass, a service in the church of St Katherine's followed by hand-washing.

Eleven o'clock was Dinner to Mathilda's relief as her stomach was always bashing her backbone by then.

A brief rest was followed by work, weaving and sewing for Mathilda as they wouldn't allow her in the gardens in case she ran away. She also had to help with washing up and sweeping up and to improve her Latin and arithmetic. Funnily enough she didn't mind this, but weaving and sewing drove her round the bend.

Five o'clock Evensong was followed by another meal, then a walk with Sister Hilda holding her, Sister Hilda who enjoyed bullying her.

Bertha loved the life. Bertha had a vocation said the nuns, proud and pleased, good Bertha. Bertha willingly did all that she was told, her eyes bent modestly on the floor. And poor Julietta did what she could, crying when she couldn't.

But it was plain that Mathilda had no vocation. She answered back, she talked when she was supposed to be silent, she hit Sister Hilda on several occasions, when her arms had been twisted just too much, and was only saved by Sister Theresa. She marched into Sister Superior's room – only Sister Theresa and Sister Christianna were allowed in – and told her the cooking was lousy and that there was no need for it as you could be good without eating rotten food. She threw her sewing across the room and shouted that they should let her out on the farm land instead. And when one of the young nuns mocked Julietta she forced her down on her knees to apologize, but Bertha reported her and she had to go down on her knees in her turn and then go without food for two days.

But these were little sins. The big ones were these:

Spitting every time she was supposed to pray for Antacill and Avelina.

Speaking in Middle English. This was the common language spoken by servants, peasants and ordinary people, the language Mathilda had grown up on with Jos and Fat Johanna. The nuns were supposed to speak Latin for prayers and at meal-times, and between themselves use Old French, the courtly language. Mathilda just spat at Old French, though her Latin was better than most, thanks to Fat Johanna.

Escaping. She was always trying to get away, and always being brought back, like a prisoner of war trying to escape from a camp. Everyone in the Priory and outside had been warned about her. She would not promise anyone not to, not even Sister Superior. And every night at prayers, she would pray out loud in Middle English that she would get away from the Priory and throw Antacill and Avelina out of the castle.

Chapter Eleven

Eyes popping out of head the manager poked and searched through Mrs Bodger's shopping trolley, but the chicken, the cake and the gateau were not there, which doesn't surprise us, but it did him, for he was sure *that boy* was guilty of something. Nor had Jason or his mother got them concealed anywhere on them. It would have been difficult for one thing. It's not easy to hide a large cooked chicken, a trifle and a gateau in your clothes unless they're very loose, and Jason and Mrs Bodger in tee-shirts and tight jeans just didn't have the room.

"Really, this is ridiculous," said Mrs Jamieson who, with Phrynne, had gone with them into the office. "There are such things as citizens' rights, you know. Mrs Bodger will send for her lawyer."

"I haven't got . . ." said Mrs Bodger.

"And I should like to use the phone so that my husband, Councillor Jamieson, can give his opinion on what's going on in here, two innocent people being treated like criminals. I shall have no hesitation in taking it further. I wonder if you know that the Chief Constable is a great friend of mine . . ."

This was not true. Mrs Jamieson had met him once

at a Parents' Evening, but Mrs J. was one who would use any weapon. And it worked.

Partly to shut her up, and partly because he really didn't know what was going on, although he was quite sure that something was, the manager opened the door for them to leave, which they did at speed, while he watched them depart mopping his brow. Was he getting old? Perhaps he needed a holiday. He'd put in for one as soon as possible.

"Let's go and have a cup of coffee," said Mrs Jamieson. "I think we deserve one."

"Please don't let anyone see me," prayed Jason as he sat in a smart café with his mother, Phrynne and her mother. He meant anyone he knew. He slumped in misery as conversation flowed over his head. And no, he didn't want a milk shake, thank you, and no, he didn't want any doughnuts, not even if they did have cream in them.

"I shall just starve and waste away until there's nothing left," he thought. "Then I shall die and she'll be happy for she'll have got me."

He meant Mathilda.

He could just see the newspaper.

Boy found dead. Mysterious circumstances. No foul play suspected. Parents and schoolmates shattered. Our finest pupil, says grieving teacher.

"And when she's got me at last she'll make me do whatever she wants and I'll be dead for ever." Again he meant Mathilda.

Tears sprang to his eyes, and he looked down at the table, feeling ready to burst with helplessness and misery.

"Why should it happen to me?" he wailed inside, as

many people have done before him and will again. And it seemed that something in his head was saying, reason, reason, there is a reason.

A hand reached out and touched him. He looked up with a sniff and Phrynne was smiling at him, not the usual mocking-sending-up-taking-the-mickey, Jason's-a-silly-idiot, a-show-off, a-boring-chauvinist-twit smile, but a dark-eyed, gentle, friendly, I'm-with-you-to-the-end-of-the-earth-or-till-Mrs Cooper-gives-us-both-detentions smile.

"I've got an idea," she said.

"It's a miracle I need," muttered Jason.

Mrs Jamieson and Mrs Bodger were quacking on, fifty words a second.

"Let's get out of here," muttered Phrynne. "Mum's awful boring."

"Mine's boring too."

They stood up.

"We're off," said Phrynne. Mrs Bodger pulled at Jason's arm.

"Jason, take care. Don't do anything strange, will you?"

"I'll look after him," said Phrynne. Jason hadn't even got the strength to protest.

"Brought down by women," he groaned to himself as he followed Phrynne to the park where they'd walked with Mrs Cooper and Mr Pridmore on that fearful afternoon when the ghost had first made her presence felt. They plonked themselves down by the

*Mynchon means a nun–so Mincinglake means nun's stream.

little rushing Mincinglake* stream and Phrynne began to talk and Jason to stuff his hands over his ears.

"No, I won't do it," he wailed, for he could still hear. You can, even if you do stuff your fingers in your ears.

"Don't be chicken . . ."

"You'd be chicken if *you* saw her. And she isn't after you, is she? No, she's after me, and she wants me, I tell you . . ."

"I'll be with you. Tell me about her and I'll manage her . . ."

"No one can. No one can manage her. I know. She's put a spell on me. I'm magicked, voodooed . . . So I don't mind being chicken. I'm going to hide where she'll never find me . . . run, run away . . "

He stood up, trembling all over. Jason, once built like a tank, now swayed like a weed blowing in the wind. Poor Jason.

"Attack is the best form of defence," said Phrynne, sounding just like Mrs Cooper.

"I don't care. I'm off. Tell them I've gone, Phrynne. Tell them for me . . ."

"Stop . . . wait . . . Jason . . ." cried Phrynne. But she was still sitting down so Jason had a fair start, and she may have been cleverer than Jason but he was much faster. As she arrived panting at the park gate, Jason had disappeared.

Jason ran as if demons were after him and perhaps they were. People stared as he hared through the narrow streets followed by cries of "Look out!", "Look where you're going!" and "Have you gone mad?"

Which in a way he had, poor old Jason. Two carrier bags went flying, and he knocked over a lanky teenager with a Mohican who was just coming out of a telephone box. He merely got to his feet and shook himself, but a nearby skinhead yelled: "Who d'you think you're pushing around?" and took off after Jason, who looked over his shoulder then ran even faster, feet hardly touching the ground, faster than he'd ever run before, his poor old brain pounding to the beat of his feet, away, away, away, running away, away, away.

"Where are you running to?" someone cried, but Jason didn't know, only what he was running from; escape from the girl, escape from his fate, escape from his doom. He had to put as many miles as possible between the Priory and himself.

By now, a policeman had spotted the skinhead, whom he knew only too well, and moved on to the trail, followed by three little kids running and a dog, and two

tenagers holding hands, sprinting, and two or three joggers.

And far, far behind all of them, ran Phrynne, terrified at last. For our Phrynne with the wicked sense of humour had found Jason and his goings-on hilarious, until at last she'd realized that something was UP, something strange and frightening, and she'd got to help for Jason might be in deadly danger. Jason would've agreed with her if he'd known her thoughts. Deadly was the word for the kind of trouble he was in.

But into his poor bewildered brain floated a picture, a view of a Cornish cliff. His holiday. That was the answer. He'd enjoyed that holiday, had fun, no ghosts had troubled him there. Cornwall. He'd head for Cornwall.

Panting now, stitch in his side, he glanced round at the skinhead who was close, much too close for comfort. What could he do? Jason swivelled his head from side to side, and saw a bike propped up against an office block. He grabbed it, leapt on it, rode, bump, bump, off the pavement on to the road and was away. This was the answer! He'd left all his pursuers behind in a moment. He pushed down the pedals strongly, standing on them to raise more power, bearing down with all his strength, hoping in some way to fight the Fate that had made all this happen to him, Jason Bodger. And as he sped along for the quickest way out of town, he thought, great, this is the way to Cornwall, I'll go by bike. I'll get away from her and everything.

He raced through the traffic lights with horns blaring and people shouting, and shot over the crossing, causing two cars to brake abruptly, then remembered too late that it was the left turning he wanted not straight on, swerved, hit the edge of the pavement, clapped on the brakes and flew over the handlebars.

As he dropped down into darkness, she came to meet him, smiling and holding out her hands, purple eyes ablaze. And all the lights in the world (and out of it) flashed and dazzled and screeched at him in red and purple and blue and yellow and green and orange and turquoise and violet and silver and gold . . . "No," screamed Jason. "No." But they bored into his brain. He couldn't shut them out. "Help me, help me," he cried.

An irritable voice in his head answered. "Help her, then. Stop messing about. Get on with it."

Chapter Twelve

The nuns said that Mathilda ws improving, that she'd settled down. But it was all camouflage. For Mathilda had begun to use her brains. She saw that being a rebel and trying to escape was a waste of time, like headbanging. Running away into those forests on her own was madness, she'd be at the mercy of whatever wild thing was there, beast, man or weather, and she wouldn't last long. What she needed was a strong loyal companion, a good horse, some weapons and provisions. For these she needed outside contacts, so she made up her mind to try to find a friend who'd get a message to the castle.

But before she could do this, visitors arrived. The Priory had quite a few, travellers and passing pilgrims or sometimes lords and ladies wanting lodging for the night. There was a special room for guests and outhouses for their servants and horses.

These guests weren't noble but they were special, Tirrell and his men. Into the entrance hall you already know, the one with fat pillars, where Jason messed about with the leaflets, were summoned Sister Christianna, Bertha, Julietta and Mathilda, who slipped in behind them, not wanting to be noticed by Tirrell. Sister Theresa was already seated there, Sister Superior being now too frail to leave her bed. Sister Hilda had also put in an unlovely appearance.

Tirrell, who was there with two soldiers, handed over a rolled-up piece of parchment sealed with a fat purple seal, intended to show it hadn't been opened on the way. In this case it wouldn't have made much difference since neither he nor his soldiers could read. Christianna read out this letter, dashing away a tear from her eye, for it said that Sir Oswald had died from wounds received on a boar hunt.

"A likely story," thought Mathilda. "I think 'orrible Anck got him."

She didn't cry for although she felt sorry, she couldn't honestly have any warm feelings about someone who'd cared so little for her. But Bertha boo-hooed loudly, followed by poor Julietta who thought this must be the right thing to do, until Sister Theresa reminded them that they should be rejoicing that their dear father was now serene in Heaven far from the sins of this world. During this, Mathilda looked out of the window where there were a couple more soldiers with the horses, one an extremely wide short soldier, who looked like – no, no it couldn't be, blessed St Anthony* of the Pigs, it just couldn't be, it wasn't possible – and then he turned round and winked at her – and it was, it was, fol-de-rol, hey nonny no, it was Segg, dear Segg, whom everyone always forgot, Segg with a daft-looking helmet on his grotty hair which had never

*A splendid Saint who loved pigs.

been combed since he was born. Mathilda nearly shrieked, nearly leapt in the air, nearly burst into tears, nearly fell about laughing, but she was more cunning these days and just smiled to herself instead. He winked again. She winked back, then lowered her eyes primly, when she felt Sister Hilda staring at her. How had he got in with Tirrell? How could she speak to him? Her thoughts went rampaging through her head like a forest fire in Australia. She'd got to get to Segg.

Christianna read on. Antacill had been installed as Lord of the Manor with great feasting and merrymaking. The celebration included rejoicing for the safe birth of his daughter, Editha. He had vowed to be a Good and Noble Lord, a Protector of his people, a Shield in their time of Trouble, and to prove this he'd had five peasants who had been found guilty of poaching and stealing wood tortured to death before an admiring audience.

He and his beloved wife Avelina trusted that their dear, dear sisters were carrying out their duties in a humble and pleasing manner. It was hoped that possibly in the future they might be visited when Bertha and Julietta were installed as nuns. Brotherly regards from Antacill and sisterly love from Avelina concluded the letter except for a P.S. which said that plans regarding Mathilda were still uncertain. Mathilda listened to all this bilge with her mind in a whirl. She'd got to see Segg. She pulled out one of the pins that held her head-dress, then stuck it sharply into Bertha's bottom.

The scream that followed nearly split the hall, and as everyone leapt and turned to see what was up,

Mathilda wailed and moaned, and fell to the floor clutching her throat, gasping and choking.

"Air, I must have air. I cannot breathe. Air, air. Let me out of here."

Bertha had jumped round and was screeching at Mathilda in a way that couldn't possibly be called humble or pleasing.

"You loathsome, plague-ridden, pestilent cow, what are you trying to do to me?"

Poor old Julietta was crying and sobbing in terror. Tirrell and his soldiers wondered what on earth they were doing among a lot of hysterical women.

"Air, air or I shall die. The plague, it must be the plague," moaned Mathilda. Now Tirrell always had instructions straight from Antacill that Mathilda must not be damaged in any way, so he thought he'd better do what the wretched girl asked. He opened the door and out stumbled Mathilda, groping, arms outstretched as if she didn't know where she was going, remembering from time to time to clutch her throat.

"Air, air," she gasped, and fell straight into Segg, who naturally didn't budge, since he was built like a tank.

"By the stream, midnight," she muttered, before pretending to pass out under a horse. And now Sister Hilda moved into action, flinging Mathilda over her shoulder in a fireman's lift – yes, I know they didn't have firemen then, but they still knew how to carry people – and carted her off to the dorter, where she intended giving her some sorting out treatment, but fortunately for Mathilda she was stopped on the way by her brother Tirrell, who warned her that this one must be specially cherished.

That night the Priory was a place of strange sounds and shadows, footsteps and whispers, of intrigue and mystery. And also, fear. A new moon, shining fitfully as clouds drifted over it, peeped through the barred windows. All appeared to be still.

But in her private cell, for she didn't sleep in the dorter along with the others, Sister Christianna was reading a piece of parchment, slipped secretly to her by one of the soldiers, when Tirrell wasn't looking. On it was written, "Mathilda must get lost. Destroy this. Your ever loving sister, Avelina."

"Well, what do you know?" murmured Christianna to herself, in Middle English, of course. Then she sat and thought and thought and thought.

In another cell Sister Theresa watched lovingly over Sister Superior, who lay dying. For the dear friend she had known and loved, Sister Theresa wept, but for the dear friend happy to leave her worn-out body for the comfort of Heaven she could only rejoice. Sister Hilda had been sent to fetch the priest. Two other nuns kept vigil with Sister Theresa, waiting for the priest and for the end of the long night. Sister Theresa prayed for Sister Superior and also for the Priory, for she feared what might happen in the future. Suppose Sister Christianna, whose ways were not those of the gentle Sister Superior, should try to take over? Sister Theresa did not like Sister Christianna. Goodness and Sister Christianna did not seem to have much in common. But would she, Sister Theresa, be strong enough to stop her? Tomorrow I shall write to the Bishop for guidance, thought Sister Theresa, leaning over to wipe the old woman's forehead.

In the dorter novice Mathilda waited. She waited for Julietta to stop kicking, for Bertha to start snoring, for Sister Isabella to start grinding her teeth, and for Sister Ludmilla to start her nightly yacking to herself, which meant that the dorter was sleeping. Where Sister Hilda had got to, she had no idea, but it was jolly lucky she wasn't around, thought our Mathilda, fixing her scratchy underblanket in a roll under her horribly scratchy overblanket with a bit of white cloth laid in position for the face. It wouldn't deceive anyone for long but it would do, for the light from the little barred windows was poor.

She crept through the dorter and out of the door, pussyfooted along a dark corridor and down the winding staircase. I'd have been terrified, but Mathilda was past being scared. If anyone stops me I'll knock 'em out, she thought. It was blacker on the ground floor, but Mathilda could manage. She entered the nuns' tiny chapel, where she'd spent many hours. Two candles burnt on the altar, and another at the statue of Our Lady, a candle for Sister Superior, but Mathilda did not know this as the young ones had not yet been told how ill she was. A small door led to the walled graveyard. Moving fast now, Mathilda climbed this wall, dropping down to the garden, then ran down to the stream.

Which was fine, everything great, only no one was there. Bent double, reed-high, so as not to be spotted, Mathilda roamed up and down the bank, getting very wet. In the end she looped up her skirts round her middle out of the way. Where was Segg? What was he messing about at, why wasn't he there? Had something happened to him? Did he know what time midnight was? You could never tell, with Segg. Perhaps he'd got drunk with the soldiers and overslept. Perhaps Tirrell had stopped him getting out. She wished he'd hurry up as she'd have to get back soon into the chapel for prayers.

And there he was. At last. A dark figure loomed up. On the other side of the stream, naturally. She whistled softly, hitched up her garments even tighter, and leapt across the stream, didn't quite make it and splashed up to her knees on the far side. She couldn't get much wetter but she did hope no one would notice later. The new moon had disappeared behind the clouds. A drizzly rain started to fall. Segg stood there, solid as an ancient monument. She tried to embrace him but since it was exactly like trying to embrace an ancient monument, she stopped.

"Are they all right? All of them? Fat Johanna? Jos? My dog, Perry?" Her voice wobbled.

Segg sounded like an ancient monument. "Yeth," he croaked. Mathilda didn't know he'd had all his teeth removed in the latest torture session, not that he'd ever been chatty.

"Out of dungeon now," he croaked on.

"Oh," cried Mathilda. "What did they do to them?"

"Yeth," answered Segg.

"Whatja mean 'Yeth'? Have you got a message for me?"

"Yeth. Come."

"Come? Where?" she hissed, peering through the now pouring rain. "Oh, you mean come to them? I know *that*. I keep trying to. But I need a horse, a friend and provisions . . ."

The rain stopped, the moon came out again and Mathilda was hit by inspiration all at the same time.

"Segg . . . can you get a horse?"

"Yeth."

"Two horses?"

"Yeth."

"Food and stuff?"

"Yeth."

"Bring them tomorrow night. Here. Right?"

"Yeth."

Mathilda thought she might as well join in.

"Yeth," she said and sprinted through the garden, over the wall, into the graveyard and into the chapel. Twice she sneezed, but she didn't worry about that.

Of course she should have left there and then, that night, when no one knew about her meeting with Segg. Poor old Mathilda. For later, at Midnight Prayers (Matins), Christianna, her head bursting with Avelina's message, could not take her eyes off her dear sister. Mathilda sneezed, not a dainty ladylike sneeze – no, not Mathilda – but a wild gnashooooo that almost lifted off the roof, and then as if that wasn't enough, she gnashoooed again, causing all the nuns to sway backwards. And Sister Christianna could see that she was soaking wet from the neck down.

Mathilda had been outside! Wandering about! She was up to something! Plotting mischief!

So Christianna sent for Sister Hilda and told her to watch Mathilda closely, without her knowing. If she went outside once more she was to follow her but not prevent her. And thus, Mathilda, tingling with excitement at the thought of escape, passing the long hours of the day waiting, was unaware that she was everywhere followed by the popping eyes of Sister Hilda.

It was a strange day, gloomy, grey and restless. During the cold, early hours just before dawn, Sister Superior had died, and now a vigil was being kept by her bedside, while prayers were said, candles lit and a fast day was proclaimed for all. But for once Mathilda did not feel hungry as she was far too busy thinking of the night and plotting her journey. There was nothing in the Priory she wished to take away with her except Fat Johanna's little book, sent as her dowry, and that was locked up in Sister Superior's cell. Mathilda had vowed that one day, however, she would return and claim it.

When night came once more she arranged the blanket roll on her bed, quite sure that Sister Hilda was at the bedside vigil. Actually S.H. was peering at her through a crack in the dorter door. Then Mathilda slipped out of the Priory and down to the stream where Segg already waited with two horses, two packs containing food, and his solid, loyal self. He also had two sharp knives and gave one to Mathilda. Old Nosey Parker Sister Hilda lay getting damp and muddy in the reeds, good, watching them go. Then she ran back and alerted Christianna.

Who sent for Tirrell in the early morning, and caught him before he left with his men on their homeward journey.

"Bring them back, but don't hurry," she told him. "There's a little job I have to do here first, so take a few days. Then I'll be ready to receive my dear, dear sister. As we all will, of course. And remember to take great care of her."

Mathilda rode through the early morning with Segg and she was singing like a bird. Oh, she was happy.

Segg had managed to tell her how they'd all been thrown into a dungeon – a dark, wet, cold, filthy, flea-ridden, pestilent, draughty dungeon complete with cobwebs, rats, spiders, slugs and so on. But the servants kept bringing them food, and Max, Jos's Dad, put everyone on a Go Slow campaign, so that no fires were lit, food cooked, farm work done etc. until the prisoners were released. 'Orrible Anck announced that he wasn't going to give into such blackmail, and told them to torture Segg. They'd begun on his teeth when, fortunately for him, a Great Lord arrived for a visit with all his retinue* and said if he wasn't properly looked after he'd let his men loose on the castle. So, very very very angry indeed, Antacill released the prisoners.

Since then, Max had been very busy organizing a Resistance movement, ready to rise up in revolt with Mathilda as their Figurehead. Her arrival back at the castle would begin the Fight.

*followers

She threw off her head-dress and her hair blew about like candy floss (which she'd never seen nor tasted). She heard the raven croak a warning, she smiled at the owl flying across her path in daylight, the kestrel dropping straight out of the sky and perching on her horse's head, the fox and the vixen who kept following them and barking at her. None of this meant a thing to her. It did to Segg. He just hoped he was getting all the warning sounds wrong. He didn't want to be captured, beaten up and tortured *again*. So he hurried Mathilda up, chivvied her along and tried to stop her singing her head off. But he was wasting his time, of course. For after being confined in the Priory with all those women, after the dorter and the Refectory, the rotten food, talking Old French and Latin, everything was now magic to Mathilda, the countryside, the blue sky, the birds, the animals, the forest, the bread and meat that Segg had brought with him (stolen).

"Going home," she sang. "I'm going home."

And after that warbled another pop song of the day called, "Mayden in the mor lay". Poor Segg sighed. A badger that should rightfully have been sleeping had just waved a paw at him and Segg was sure it was trying to tell him something.

It was. They had covered quite a few miles when once more Tirrell and his militia surrounded them.

"This is getting monotonous," Segg thought as he knocked out three of them. But there were too many, and he was thrown to the ground and stamped on a few times.

"Sorry," said Tirrell to Mathilda. And she went

bananas with fury. Still on her horse, scarlet with temper, she rode at the soldiers trampling poor old Segg, and knocked them flying in surprise. Then she turned and charged straight at Tirrell the Terror, knife held high in her hand.

"Ouch," he yelled as she got him in the arm. She whirled her horse around and rushed at him again, hair flying like a strawberry cloud, eyes wide.

"I'll make pork chops of you," she shrieked and meant it. Tirrell was almost afraid for a moment, but she was very small and he was a large man for those days. The fight didn't last long. Besides, his soldiers backed him up.

"Sorry," he repeated, as one of them clonked her on the back of her head. And he meant it in a way. He was getting to admire Mathilda. Almost . . . almost . . . he thought he wouldn't mind fighting for her instead of Antacill, but he soon got rid of such a daft idea and had his arm fixed up instead. Segg and Mathilda were tied up and draped over horses to be carted back to the Priory rather like badly wrapped parcels being returned to sender.

Sister Christianna awaited them in her cell, seated on a new chair, with Sister Hilda standing behind her.

"What are you doing here?" shrieked Mathilda, conscious once more but with a large bump on her head, which was covered once more with a head-dress. "You've no right to be here. Where's Sister Theresa? I want Sister Theresa."

As she cried and wept, waves of heat shook her,

followed by a shivering chill, for the fever had stricken Mathilda, working on the theory that since everything looked so rotten for her it might as well be a bit worse. "Fetch Sister Theresa, you beastly cow."

"I'm sorry to say that Sister Theresa had an accident and we decided that it was best for her to have a little holiday, so she is no longer with us," said Sister Superior Christianna. "Moreover, since I am now the Sister Superior here, my word is law and you must treat me with respect."

"What have you done with her, you old bag? I'll get you for this if it's the last thing I do."

"I don't know about your getting me, but you're certainly about to do your last thing," said Sister Christianna.

Mathilda began to scream and shout, enormous shudders and shivers almost breaking her in two.

"Gag her," said Christianna coldly.

Tirrell didn't want to. One of the soldiers did it.

"Hey, you do know she isn't to be damaged. The Lord Antacill was most insistent," said Tirrell apprehensively.

"The orders have been changed. Take her to the dorter and wall her up. Then you report back to the castle that she was lost escaping in the forest. Here is a ring for your pains and some silver for the soldiers."

The ring was Julietta's dowry.

And so the soldiers began their work, walling up Mathilda in a corner of the dorter. They didn't like it much and they protested but not enough. Mathilda could not cry for help and as she flung herself against the rapidly rising wall the merciful fever took over and she fell to the floor. She tried to bang and to scream but couldn't, and anyway everyone had been moved out of that part of the Priory while building operations were carried out.

At last quiet settled and Mathilda stirred in a blackness. A long time passed and she felt very hungry and then not hungry. Somewhere a voice spoke but she couldn't hear what it said, something about a mix-up but she didn't understand that and drifted into darkness once more, and again . . . and again . . . and again . . . and again . . . and again . . .

And opened her eyes. The gag had gone and her hands were free. And the wall was down. She didn't know why. Perhaps now she could escape. But she would need help. Segg had been there, she remembered. Where was Segg now? She'd better investigate. Everything looked rather hazy, and she was a bit dizzy after that nasty fever, though that might be because she was so thin and hungry. She thought she'd been hungry for ever.

She must make a start on getting out of here. She began to walk across the dorter floor and looked across to where there was a railing that she couldn't remember, and some rubbish lying on the other beam. Strange that, for the Priory was always so tidy and clean.

Who were all those people? What were they wearing? How peculiar they looked. But–but–look who was there with them! It couldn't be. But it was. In very weird clothes indeed. It must be a disguise. He'd come in a disguise and brought all those people to help her. Dear Jos. Good old Jos. He'd come to save her. She knew he would. She knew Jos would not let her stay walled up for . . . ever.

Holding out her hands she hurried towards him, smiling, telling him how awful everything had been and how happy she was now that he'd come for her at last . . .

Chapter Thirteen

Something was pressing heavily on Jason. It was hard to move. In fact he didn't want to move and he lay there for some time thinking about not wanting to move. When at last he cautiously shoved out a leg to the side of the bed, he found out why. Oh, he ached. Oh, how he ached. Just as if he'd been run over by a steam roller. Run over! The bike, he remembered the bike! And with that –

"Ow!" screamed Jason. "Is she there? Has she got me?"

The girl at the side of the bed smoothed his head. "No, it's me. Not the ghost."

"Oh, Phrynne, oh, Phrynne, I'm glad it's you."

Phrynne went a bit pink.

"That's the nicest thing you've ever said to me."

His mother sat on the other side of the bed.

"Frynay rang for the ambulance. Got you back here. She's been ever so good."

"She's called Frin, not Frynay," said Jason crossly. "Can I get up now?" He tried. "Ooh, ooh. Ouch!"

"Better stay put," said his mother. "Go back to sleep."

"Stay here with me, Phrynne. Keep her away."

"Poor Jason, you're delirious. The doctor says you must stay in bed for at least a couple of days," said his mother.

"I'll stay," said Phrynne.

They didn't tell him that the police wanted to question him about a stolen and crashed bike. The doctor had said that must wait till he was stronger and this was yet more trouble in store. But for the moment he slept and Phrynne sat beside the bed reading an old History book her mother had found. One chapter in it was all about a certain Priory, called St Katherine's . . . And then she read on in yet another book her mother had lent her all about nunneries and priories. A nunnery (or priory) could be a vocation, a career, a refuge or . . . a prison.

"Vocation," thought Phrynne. "That's something you want to do more than anything else, something you're called to do. Career's a job – that's all right. A refuge, that's a place where someone in danger would feel safe. But a prison, ugh," she shuddered, and read on.

"Sometimes young girls who weren't wanted by their families were put in these houses, sometimes girls who were deformed or mad . . . Oh, no, poor things," thought Phrynne. She read the little rhyme on the page.

"Now earth to earth in convent walls,
To earth in churchyard sod.
I was not good enough for man
And so am given to God."

Underneath that was written, "A young nun, Mathilda de Chetwynde, was put in a priory at eleven.

But she escaped and married and was pardoned by the Pope."

"Mathilda de Chetwynde," thought Phrynne, "Mathilda de Chetwynde . . . the name makes me feel funny. I wonder . . . but it couldn't be . . . else she would've already escaped and not be . . . a ghost . . . would she? Oh, I can't work it out, it's . . . too . . . much . . . for . . ."

"Frynay," Mrs Bodger was shaking her gently. "Wake up, Frynay, it's late. Your mother's come to fetch you. Thank you, Frynay."

"Frin," said that girl. "I'll be back tomorrow."

As Jason recovered Phrynne talked. Jason tried not to listen. But Phrynne made him. She told him she was sure that the ghost was a young nun called Mathilda de Chetwynde and that she was trying to escape from the Priory and for some reason she needed Jason's help.

"You must go to the Priory and find *her*. Instead of her always coming after you. I know it."

"No, no, no, no, no."

"It's the only way to find out what it's all about."

"I don't want to know what it's all about."

"Then she'll go on popping up after you all over the place and you'll turn into a nervous wreck."

"I'm a nervous wreck now."

"You mean a ghost of your former self." (I told you Phrynne's sense of humour was diabolical.)

"Don't say that. That's what scares me."

"What?"

"That I'll end up a . . . what you said. Oh, Phrynne, help me."

"I will if you'll do what I say. We've got to go back to the Priory."

"You ain't got any nerves, have you?" said Jason bitterly.

"She's just a girl. I can cope with girls, dead or alive."

"I can't. Don't want to."

"Then you'll have to go on like this."

"No."

"Tomorrow, then."

"No." Jason turned pale. "Next week, Phrynne. Perhaps she won't come again. Give me a few more days."

"All right. But soon."

That night he dreamed. The ghost beamed down on to the bottom of his bed, sat down, stuck out her sandalled feet and smiled at him, holding out her hands, beseechingly. He put his head under his pillow and cried.

"I'll come," he said to Phrynne next day when she came round after school. Jason hadn't been to school which seemed far away these days. Once it was the most important thing in his whole life, now he could hardly remember it. He'd spent his days at home resting, watching telly and . . . reading a book from the library on Life in the Middle Ages . . . Mrs Cooper wouldn't have believed it. He looked very pale. Phrynne peered at him closely and then called to his mother.

"We're just going for a walk, Mrs Bodger."

"Are you sure you're all right, Jason?" she asked, hurrying in.

"He'll be fine," answered Phrynne, and out they

walked into the sunshine. It had been the best ever summer for nearly everyone except Jason, who now walked like one in a dream, or a nightmare rather, Phrynne beside him, pretending to be much braver than she actually felt. They took a few moments crossing the dangerous road where Jason had once thumbed his nose at a lorry driver, but that was a different boy from this one, and all the cars drew up to let them pass. On they went through the park and there walking towards them was Mr Pridmore, teaching practice over.

"Why, Phrynne and Jason, hello. How are you?"

Jason didn't answer, but said suddenly: "Come with us. Please come with us. To the Priory."

Mr Pridmore was astonished as well he might be at the thought of Jason asking him to go anywhere, but he wasn't doing anything special and he fancied seeing the Priory again. They'd left in such a hurry last time. Besides, Jason looked pale and peculiar and some very funny stories had been circulating about him in school, making Mr Pridmore curious.

"I'll come. I'll be glad to. I shall enjoy this."

Phrynne twitched and Jason looked as if he was going to throw up, but on they went through the park, brown and dusty now with the sun and no rain.

"Shall we all have an ice-cream? And do call me Anthony," he said as they came out of the park and into the narrow streets.

"No thank you, Mr Pridmore," said Phrynne. Jason didn't even answer.

"You're hundreds of miles away," Mr Pridmore joked feebly.

But Jason wasn't. He was hundreds of years away, or on his way there. For Jason had stopped fighting against Fate, struggling against his doom, and was off to do what he had to, caught in a dream/time bubble. On they walked through the streets together, Mr Pridmore, Phrynne and Jason, and it seemed that traffic stopped for them, people smiled and moved out of their way and a little breeze helped them along, making Mr Pridmore very nervous since he was used to things going wrong all of the time. Once they all stopped together and smiled at each other for no reason at all.

The Priory was almost empty for the tourists were leaving for tea. Mr Pridmore had just the right money for the tickets.

"Have a nice look round," said the curator, a new one, a very pretty girl. Up the stairs they climbed to the place where Jason had first encountered the ghost of a nun.

It was all still. Far below the kitchen was dark and silent and old. The dusty paper plates still lay on the beam.

The three of them stood by the railings and waited. Nothing happened. Jason turned to Phrynne.

"What now?" he asked.

"Just tell her you've come. And that I'll be with you."

Jason smiled at her almost pityingly, and turned away.

"But you won't be, Phrynne. It's just me, you see," and he held out his hands towards the beam and called out, "Mathilda, ich come."

As Mr Pridmore and Phrynne stared at him the air stirred and quivered, shimmering like a heat haze, but cold not hot. There was a rushing sound, and the far-off echo of a voice answering. Phrynne wanted to cry, to laugh. She felt sad, triumphant, wild, happy all at once. And then all she could do was to hold tight to the railing as the Priory rocked on its foundations. Far, far away a voice cried: "Steady on. Less power. Please."

Everything went quiet. Phrynne grabbed Mr Pridmore to get some comfort but he was green and shaking, more scared than she was, so she held him instead.

Jason stretched out his arm.

"I've got to go over there," he said.

Phrynne looked at the chewed and ancient beam, the dusty plates.

"It's not safe," she screamed.

"The floor's perfectly safe," said Jason in a robot voice. Then he stepped forward. Not on to the beam they could see but on to the one they couldn't. Into nothingness. Phrynne wailed and closed her eyes. Mr Pridmore shouted, "Jason! You'll be killed!"

But Jason was walking away from them, fast and then faster, holding out his hands to who or whatever was waiting for him.

And disappeared.

Phrynne was sobbing as if her heart would break, as indeed she thought it would with terror and misery.

"I wanted to go, go, too," she howled, tears spurting all over Mr Pridmore's shirt.

"Would you mind telling me just what's going on here?" said a large voice. The little curator had arrived, with a large policeman in tow.

"That's them," she said breathlessly. "The three of them. And then the place went mad. So I fetched you."

"Three of them? I can only see two," said the fuzz, taking out his notebook. "D'you mind telling me where the other one's got to? The one we've already got our eyes on. Supermarket trouble. Stolen bicycles. Where is he? What's he up to?"

Phrynne and Mr Pridmore looked at each other in despair.

"And I'll start by taking your names."

"Why did I ever come here?" thought Mr Pridmore. "I should have known that anything to do with Jason Bodger would be a disaster."

"Phrynne Jamieson," that girl was saying, between sobs.

"Come on, Miss. What sort of name is that? Frin? Your proper name please . . ."

The questioning went on for hours, poor Mr Pridmore sunk in misery, thinking what a fool he'd been to get mixed up again with Jason Bodger. Phrynne cried.

Mrs Jamieson, Mrs Bodger, Mrs Cooper were all called together and oh dear, what a caffuffle and carry-on there was. Kids and grown-ups all agreed that Jason Bodger had been steadily going barmy all that term, and there was mention of a stolen bicycle and food from supermarkets. It didn't look good. The Priory was closed to visitors while it was thoroughly investigated. Nothing was found.

DISAPPEARANCE OF JASON BODGER.
One of life's unsolved mysteries?

asked the headline in the daily paper.

Everyone appeared in turn and sometimes together on local TV and radio. Mr Pridmore actually appeared on National TV. He didn't want to but at least he got three offers of a job as a result. He'd made forty applications up till then and heard nothing. A bit of him thought maybe knowing Jason Bodger wasn't so bad after all.

Phrynne claimed she was Jason's girl-friend and went round saying that after knowing him she wouldn't marry anyone else *ever*. Mrs Cooper said nothing, but left for the Isle of Skye on a long holiday.

Chapter Fourteen

Just as Mathilda reached Jos, who was really Jason, and pulled at his sleeve, everything went black . . .

"A plague on this fever," she muttered as she came round later, then managed a faint shadow of a giggle as she realized what she'd said.

"I've got to do something? What was it?" Her poor brain felt tired and slow, jet-lagged, though she wouldn't have known the term. Jos, she'd seen Jos. Jos was about here, somewhere. By some miracle he'd managed to get into the Priory, with all those funny-looking people, talking in strange voices. Still, he was there, that was the main thing. Find him and Segg and she could make her escape. She must escape . . . She must escape . . . She must escape . . . The blackness descended once more.

Coming round yet again, she felt much better, got out of bed and crept quietly towards the main Priory door. Everywhere was peaceful and deserted which was because the tourists hadn't arrived as yet, not that she knew. A new nun in very weird clothes sat in the hall but she was looking at something peculiar, and Mathilda didn't stop to find out because all she wanted was freedom.

She stepped out of the door. And closed her eyes. And closed her ears. For the fever was giving her hallucinations. Where was she? Where was the grass? What had happened to the trees? All those horrible castles everywhere. What were those ugly noises, banging and snarling? And the dusty smells that caught her breath? A tall thin monster walked by on long, scraggy legs, wearing wire bits on its head. Music came from a box it carried. She started to run down the alleyway and found that she could glide instead. She turned a corner, then hid trembling behind it, for coloured shiny boxes shot everywhere, throwing out smoke and roaring like animals.

"Is it a dream? Or am I very ill?" thought Mathilda. And found she could fly and hover above all the boxes and the buildings and the tall, peculiar people everywhere, more than she'd ever seen at one time.

She didn't know what she was doing, but this gliding was pleasant and she could take a good look round for Jos and then get back to home, the castle where things were green and ordinary. Oh, that awful noise above her head as she glided along above the boxes and people! A great bird whirred in the sky – it could only come from hell, it was so frightening. A hellibird. Take no notice of it. That was best. Just find Jos and Segg and get away. They'd help her sort everything out. On she glided.

Something seemed to be pulling her along to a large sprawling building with green grass round one side of it. The green grass looked very nice and she landed on it.

She peered through long windows into a large room where lots of children were messing about on pieces of wood. And among them was Jos! Dear Jos! Though what he was doing there when he was supposed to be helping her, Mathilda, she had no idea. Through the windows she flew, and since she didn't know about glass, she didn't realize she'd just gone straight through some. Ignoring everyone else she swung towards Jos on a large branch, telling him to come and join her, to help her. But Jos seemed to be very upset about something and just as she was about to ask why, the blackness seized her again and all was still.

Coming to, she groped around her, for the horrible wall had grown once more and she was so hungry, so very hungry, starving . . . to death . . . she mustn't think about that, no. All the Mathildaness in her, the power, the love of life, of being Mathilda, rose up and protested. No, she was not going to die in this miserable, squitty fashion, not she, not Mathilda. Using fantastic will power she pushed with all her strength against the dreadful wall, and it gave way before her. She lay for a while exhausted in the dorter, then glided forth into that noisy world outside, that place of madness.

And landed on the food counter. Hungry as she was, she threw herself upon the gorgeous grub. It was all quite different from ordinary food, but after the Priory cooking it was Heaven. Nearly as good as Fat Johanna's. Fat Johanna. Would she ever see her again? Don't think about that. Eat up the food. Fill the empty tum. Perhaps the fact that she hadn't eaten for so long was why everything seemed so strange, for she wasn't seeing things properly. She'd almost given up hope of anything appearing normal or ordinary. The whole world had changed, and all she could hope for was to get back to the castle. And now she was so weak and wobbly, she needed Jos to help her, more than ever, Jos do come, please. Jos, come and find me, come, come, come and help me, please.

And there he was, of course, walking towards her, looking mulish and stupid, together with an older boy, or no, could it be a woman? She was wearing trousers and she didn't look much like a woman, thought Mathilda, but what Jos was doing walking around with her, she couldn't imagine. He looked big and tough, a good thing. Jos would need to be strong.

She rammed down some more food, already feeling better. This time she'd sort it all out, and escape from the Priory. There was a good deal of fussing going on, people shouting and so on. A black-haired boy had joined Jos. What was Jos doing mixed up with all these people? She tried to speak to him, but he just looked bewildered. Oh dear. A dizzy feeling swept over her as she stuck out a tongue at the black-haired boy who'd just pointed at her in a rude way, and then she was whirled away.

Time blurred. She moaned to herself: "Come, Jos, come, if I don't go soon it will be too late . . . too late . . ."

Time passed. She woke and slept, woke and slept until one day . . . there he was at last, walking towards her looking as if he could solve anything. Not looking scared, not running away from her, but saying: "Mathilda, ich come."

There followed a great deal of noise and confusion and she thought the Priory would collapse around them, but somehow they made their way through blurred walls and shifting stairs to the outside world, an outside world green and quiet once more with grass and fields where waited Segg with soldiers and horses. She turned, full of hope and happiness to Jos, and startled, cried: "But you're not Jos!"

"Well, I never said I was, did I?" answered Jason Bodger. "Who's he, anyway?"

Chapter Fifteen

"But I'm not dead," snapped Mathilda as they rode along. "It's you that's not right in the head."

She spoke in Middle English and Jason answered in the same. Gloomily.

"You've been dead for centuries, you 'ave. About seven or eight. That's a long time."

"Don't be so stupid, fleabag that you are, boar fleabag. You can see I'm not dead. Look. I'm here. And it's now. And I'm real. Pinch my arm. Ouch! You didn't have to pinch that hard. You are one of the mad people, one of the funnies. If I were cruel like my sisters I'd have you locked up. But I'm nice, I am. Don't pull that face. I'm very nice. And I shall be a great Lady, stop laughing won't you? Whereas you'll be a barmy prophet, that people come for miles to see because you say crazy things and make them laugh with all that stuff about horseless chariots and carts and machines in the sky that fly like birds . . ."

"You saw those yourself!! You admitted it."

"It was a dream. When I was ill with the fever."

"No, it was for real, I tell you. And there's other things, telly and cassettes and telecom and computers and nukes . . ." He stopped there. He didn't much want to tell Mathilda about nukes.

"What are nukes? Take that cross look off your face and tell me. Go on."

"Nukes," said Jason slowly, "are very powerful weapons that can blow up the world, kill everything, all of us."

"Weapons like spears? Catapults? Bows and arrows?"

"No, not like them. Worse. Dangerous. To us all."

"Can I have one for the castle? To kill Antacill?"

"No, because it would kill everyone in your castle and forests, all people and animals as well, so it wouldn't be any use, for we'd be dead too."

"What a silly weapon. What use is that? Hundreds of years did you say? It took that long time to make rubbish like that? They must be all very stupid in your time, like you."

Jason rode on in silence. Segg and the soldiers followed behind. The journey back to the castle was long and wearisome and gave Jason and Mathilda lots of time to argue. They enjoyed arguing.

"If," said Mathilda, "you are really an in-our-time person, you are barmy, and if not, you are the future for we are here *now*."

"I'm the *now* person," shouted Jason. "I'm modern. You're gone, you are. Past it."

"I'm not past it," shrieked Mathilda. "Do I look past it?"

Candy-floss hair floated through the air, and she was golden with sunshine. She looked marvellous, the Middle Ages' answer to Miss World.

"No, you look great. But you're still dead."

"I am not," Mathilda hissed through her teeth, "dead. You haven't happened yet."

"I'm here, aren't I? So I must have happened," growled Jason.

After a peevish five minutes she asked: "Why do you speak like us, since you aren't one of us?"

"Telepathy."

"What?"

"Don't you know anything? Brain messages passed without any words. Our brains are translating what we're both saying. Like my jeans and tee-shirt have been changed into these scum-bag, flea-bitten clothes."

"You look better than you did in that stuff before."

"When you were a ghost, you mean."

"I was *not* a ghost. I was ill and seeing things strangely."

"When I met you, you were a ghost begging me to help you, just a bit of old History. You don't seem like a ghost now but you are, because your time has really gone . . ."

"Jason, you may be crazy like a hermit or a wise man, I don't know, but I'll race you to that tree and win."

She did, of course. Jason arrived second, panting. She grinned at him.

"You person in the future, you will stay and help me fight for the castle? You won't want to go back, will you?"

"I might."

"Why?"

"There's football and telly and junk food and a girl named Phrynne."

"A what?"

"A girl. You put your tongue out at her."

"Oh, that nasty, black-haired boy."

"Not a boy. Phrynne."

"What is the noise you make? Yuk. Phrynne, yuk."

"Yuk to you, too."

"Stay with me and we shall rule the castle."

Segg spoke, as he did once in a while.

"Ee ath ooo athtoo ee verth," meaning they'd got to capture it first. And of course, they had to. For despite all the arguments and mad rides through the woods, Antacill still had to be dealt with.

As they made their way through the forest, people came out to join them, in ones and twos at first, then more and more, emerging from hidden places, sliding from the huge trees, riding along the quiet paths, all falling in behind Mathilda and her band, a mini-army gathering out of hatred for Antacill and all tyrants who make ordinary people's life a misery. In their hands they carried sticks and staves, long poles and farm tools. But there were others, with a harder look in their eyes, who carried knives and bows and arrows, the professionals who travelled the country looking for trouble-spots to join in and earn themselves a little gold and booty. To Jason they nearly all looked squat and short, and many had rotten teeth or an arm or leg missing. But they laughed and smiled and shouted for Mathilda, and here and there he caught sight of a face that seemed familiar, the image of one he knew in his

own later world, one who looked like his uncle, another like Mr Pridmore, only about a foot shorter.

They sang and joked as they journeyed along until Castle Adamant loomed over the forest trees, and then they fell silent. Together they gathered in a wooded valley, well concealed by the giant yew trees that ringed it.

"We must plan our attack," announced Mathilda, perched high on a fallen tree.

Pandemonium followed as about three hundred and fifty people put forward four hundred ideas.

At last Segg uttered. "Uth," he cried and everyone fell silent.

A tall thin man with the face of an animal-trap stepped forward.

"This is how we captured a castle up north," he said and outlined a plan.

Mathilda listened, then looked at him for a long time.

"To fight Antacill with you would be to use poison against poison. But I have no fight with you. Only take your men away, for we are not your kind. Find another war."

Two dozen camouflaged men slid quietly out of the valley and disappeared.

"That's a pity," Jason muttered. "He'd got the right ideas."

"Don't worry. I'm not an idiot," said Mathilda. "I've noted the ideas. It's him we don't want."

A figure made its way down into the middle of the valley to where Mathilda perched on her tree. Jason stared, as well he might.

Jos had arrived.

Antacill had fortified the castle. All the little wattle and daubs outside had been burnt, the animals seized, and the people driven into the forest where, of course, they joined Mathilda. The drawbridge was drawn up over the moat, and the castle crammed with Tirrell and his men, boiling oil on the parapet, plus great wooden catapults and slings for heaving massive boulders at the enemy, bows and arrows in the slits and behind the battlements. Animals and provisions were gathered up and water very important – was laid on. Antacill was in complete Control with Tirrell Second. On the top of the castle stood two stakes, to which Max and Fat Johanna were tied tightly. Peredoc lay protectingly over Fat Johanna's feet. The castle waited.

But Jos had escaped from this, had crept out before it hotted up too much. For months he'd been building up a cache of weapons for the Great Day of Mathilda's Return, and he'd got a pretty hot collection. You remember I told you he was keen on weapons and knew his stuff – bows and arrows, long bows, spears, lances, swords, knives, arquebuses (whatever they are), some ropes and scaling ladders, all the lot. He was proud of it and dying for Mathilda to arrive so he could show it off.

But on seeing Jason he stopped dead, immediately macho, like a turkey-cock. Jason stood up and stared back.

They were not identical. Jason was taller, Jos broader, Jason had blue eyes, Jos brown, but both were tanned, both tough, and you'd mistake one for the other if you didn't look closely.

"Who's ee?" asked Jos, jabbing his thumb at Jason.

"Not sure, mate," drawled Jason. "But I think you might be my great-great-great grandad."

"Eh?" asked Jos.

"Take no notice," put in Mathilda. "He's mad, but he's on our side and he'll help us."

According to custom it should have been early dawn when Mathilda and her troops attacked but Jason hadn't watched modern tactics and the SAS on the telly for nothing. It was blackest night when the castle was surrounded by men camouflaged with leaves, bracken, dirt. Jos's cache of weapons had been shared out among them.

The main problem was getting into the castle, standing high, remote and seemingly impregnable on its hill, the dark, still, icy waters of the moat all around it.

And into the moat in the small, mean hours of the morning slipped three dark figures, Mathilda (hair screwed up under a cap), Jos and Jason. For Mathilda and Jos knew every inch of the Castle as well as they knew the forest, and just above the water-line, hidden by a huge flowery bush growing over it was an opening, too small for a man to squeeze through. But these three could. The water was so cold it bit right through to the bone, especially Jason's bones, as he wasn't so used to hardship as the other two. The three hardly rippled the water as they swam across, then crawled under the branches into the castle cellar, crammed full with food, animals and drink. Carefully they crept through these obstacles and up a winding staircase and into the great empty banqueting hall that led towards the main courtyard, where half a dozen soldiers were on guard, two by the drawbridge, two patrolling and two playing cards at a trestle table.

"And now," hissed Mathilda. Jos and Jason pulled on their masks (wet and yucky but they didn't notice they were so scared/excited), and Mathilda flung off her cap and threw out her yards of hair and began to move. As Jason had once said, that girl was a right mover.

"Look at me, look at me, look at me," she screamed at the very top of her voice, and they did – all the soldiers, bored and half asleep, woke up with a wow, caw look at that, get that, grab it, me, no me, why it's her, HER, get it, the boss'll want it, capture it, move, after her . . .

And Mathilda, hair flying, legs leaping, arms waving, was doing the lot, tango, sambo, disco, jive, bopping faster than had ever been done before in the old castle, and as she danced and screeched, "Can't catch me stupids," and "She loves you yeah, yeah, yeah," a chorus from the Beatles which she'd heard on a transistor briefly and couldn't forget, she headed for the main staircase, soldiers streaming after her, arms outstretched to grab, with her always just ahead.

Moving like robots, Jason and Jos rushed to the drawbridge, and smoothly and quickly began to lower it (Jos had told Jason all about the way it worked), while Mathilda led the soldiers further and further away up the stairs, enjoying herself no end for she loved showing off and here was a good audience. They'd forgotten all about the drawbridge, specially as she started to sing a few insults as well, fat belly, and flat feet, and warty, and wobble gob, as she went, as they all went. Her plan – oh, brave Mathilda – was to lead them right to the very top of the castle and leap off down into the moat and back to Segg and company, who would be, in fact even now were, rushing in over the drawbridge with ear-splitting shouts, sounding like the end of the world. Archers were lined on the banks opposite ready to shoot as soon as Mathilda was safely over and back into the moat. Behind them were dozens of kids and at a signal they all began to bang and shout and sing and scream as loud as they could. Surprise, as their professional had said, is the best weapon.

Inside the courtyard, hand-to-hand fighting had already begun, with swords and knives and sticks, for four of the soldiers had realized what was up and turned round from Mathilda, calling for the others who were sleeping. Boiling oil was thrown from the top but most of the invaders had safely crossed the drawbridge by now, and it didn't go far enough to drench the archers on the far side. Tirrell, roused from sleep, and in a fiendish temper, rushed out shouting directions, and Antacill and Avelina woke up, each blaming the other for whatever was going on, as they grabbed their clothes, ready to fight in Antacill's case, in Avelina's to seize her jewels and baby (in that order) and get ready to join whoever won, or possibly to escape if she needed to.

"Do what I say," commanded Antacill from the top

of the stairs down into the courtyard but no one took a blind bit of notice, being too busy doing their own thing with the particular enemy they'd lined up.

Jason and Jos were fighting back to back, for they'd already found they worked well as a team, and that way they were in no danger of a stab from the rear. Segg, like a giant oak, armed with a huge stave laid about him right, left and centre. Shouts and blows re-echoed through the banqueting hall and slowly the invaders gained their objectives.

Bursting with rage, Antacill leapt up and down, cursing and shouting, and was knocked over by Tirrell chasing an invader.

"It's chaos," he shouted. "A muddle."

"Always is," yelled Tirrell, "see if you can see what's going on from the top."

And so it was that Antacill reached the castle roof and spotted Mathilda. She should already have jumped off into the moat but as she ran across she saw Fat Johanna gagged and bound with Peredoc whining at her feet. He wanted to join the battle but didn't want to leave her. And Max too, gagged and bound. Tears spurting from her eyes, Mathilda cut away the ropes as fast as she could with Peredoc leaping all over her, and by then it was too late to jump for the noise of battle was all over the castle and Tirrell's soldiers tried to hold their own.

"Down the stairs," yelled Max, who wanted to be where it was all happening. And Antacill saw Mathilda. With one leap he seized her, twisted her in front of him and pointed a dagger at her throat. And just then, Jos and Jason, with Segg hard on their heels, arrived.

"One false move," said Antacill, "and she dies."

"Give up," said Jos.

"You've lost, you 'orrible-looking man," said Jason.

"So surrender," said Jos.

"Let her go," said Jason.

"I do the bargaining," said Antacill, smiling. "I want two horses, with food and provisions brought to the drawbridge for me, and then I want a twenty-four-hour truce for us to leave for France. One false move on your part and she dies. If you behave sensibly she shall go safely with me and be my bride."

Mathilda bit him. But though he flinched and blood flowed, he didn't let go. Back against the parapet, Mathilda held tight against him, he waited.

The others waited too, faces blank. For up behind him, mounting high on a scaling ladder, appeared the gap-toothed face of Segg, a huge stave in his hand.

Plonk, it scrunched down on Antacill's head and he fell flat on his face while Mathilda quickly wriggled away. He would be out cold for some time as was anyone hit by Segg.

Tirrell, arriving at the top, saw his master lying prone, and summed up the situation in a flash, going down on his knees to Mathilda, saying: "I am your loyal servant to the end."

"That depends whose end it is, I suppose," said Mathilda. "Oh, all right. But go and stop the rest of the fighting and round people up so that Max here can sort it all out. And find my sister, Avelina."

The part of Leader came naturally to Mathilda. She walked down to the banqueting hall, followed by the others, and sat on the main chair, with Fat Johanna and her, Jos and Jason on her left, Max on her right. The people and soldiers assembled, rounded up by Tirrell, working hard as usual.

"Where is my sister?" asked Mathilda.

"I think she escaped down a scaling ladder. Since she had the baby people let her through. Do you want me to follow and kill her?"

"No, of course not. See that she goes to the Priory, where Sister Theresa will be in charge from now on. She'll either reform Avelina or she and Christianna will drive each other crazy. Put Antacill in a dungeon for now. He can help with Community Work later. All the village huts have to be rebuilt and stocked. There's a lot to do."

She turned to the people waiting.

"First we'll have a feast. Then we'll get to work. Remember I'm the Boss."

She looked at Jason and grinned. "OK?" She'd learnt that off Jason.

And everyone cheered.

Chapter Sixteen

Time passed.

Jason wasn't sure how long.

And then one morning he woke up remembering the League Table and the charts. And more than anything else in the world he wanted to know who was TOP. He wanted to go home, he told Jos and Mathilda.

"Don't go. Please don't go," said Mathilda.

"Stay here with us," said Jos. "No need to go."

"I've got to. Just got to. Besides, a voice in my head keeps telling me to go back or it'll muck up History."

"When?" asked Mathilda, not messing about.

"Now. It means going to the beam in the Priory. Come with me, you two."

"I can't," said Mathilda. "Antacill comes to trial next week."

"I'll come with you," said Jos.

Segg went as well. It took a long time, as usual. Jason explained about jets and rockets, high speed trains and racing cars on the way.

"I'd like to use a computer," said Jos. "And fly a plane."

Sister Theresa welcomed them and asked for all the news.

"Sometimes the sisters are tiresome, but little Julietta is a good girl. We're happy here."

Jos and Jason went up to the dorter. Jos watched Jason walk on to the beam.

Jason stretched out his arms and cried, "Take me back, please." And covered his head with his arms as the Priory shook and trembled and lightning flashed through the dark room. A throbbing and humming like machinery filled the air, growing louder, louder . . . louder . . . LOUDER . . .

Jos, crouched low, cried: "Goodbye, friend and . . ." . . . and was whirled away.

Jason's arms stretched out again in shock this time and he heard a voice – the one he'd heard before. The voice groaned.

"Oh no! Not again! You've messed it up, you blithering idiot. You've got the wrong one."

And Jos arrived in the middle of Class 4z standing with Mrs Cooper and Mr Pridmore in front of a railing overlooking the old kitchen at the Priory. Several plates and cups lay on the one chewed-up old beam in front of them.

Other Puffins by Gene Kemp

GOWIE CORBY PLAYS CHICKEN

Gowie Corby is the trouble-maker in his class, but his life is revolutionized by black American Rosie Angela Lee. A very funny and unexpectedly touching story.

THE TURBULENT TERM OF TYKE TILER

Tyke's championship of Danny Price is at the bottom of most of the happenings in class 4M of Cricklepit Combined School. Fast, funny, with a surprise ending, this book won the Carnegie Medal and the Other Award.

CHARLIE LEWIS PLAYS FOR TIME

Cricklepit Combined School, which produced Tyke Tiler and endured Gowie Corby, is now coping with five of the numerous Moffat family. Trish and the others find they have a new teacher for their last term at Cricklepit, a strict disciplinarian who believes in silence, segregation and sex discrimination. But for one member of the family the worst thing is that Mr Carter has a passion for music.

THE CLOCK TOWER GHOST

Addlesbury Tower is haunted by Rich King Cole and its newest terror is Mandy – feared by her family and eventually by the Clock Tower Ghost too.

DOG DAYS AND CAT-NAPS

A delightful assortment of animal stories, featuring dogs and cats and the odd gerbil. Each story is just the right length for reading at a single sitting.

JUNIPER

Most people live happily ever after, or that's how it seems to Juniper. But since her dad left she's had nothing but problems – there are even threats to put her into care. Then she notices two suspicious men who seem to be following her. Who are they? Why are they interested in her? As Christmas draws nearer, Juniper knows something is going to happen . . .

NO PLACE LIKE
(for older readers)

Pete Williams just wants to be left alone. An impossibility, since he lives with a larger-than-life father, a mother who is convinced that Pete has 'problems' and a sister who is bright, attractive and clever. When Pete starts his new college he finds himself in the trendy group and suddenly his life is taken over by a succession of discos, parties – and something more sinister in the form of Oliver and Kenny. And then, of course, there was the girl . . .